P9-BAV-797

Just Friends

Novels by Dyan Sheldon

Confessions of a Teenage Drama Queen

Confessions of a Teenage Hollywood Star

The Crazy Things Girls Do for Love

I Conquer Britain

My Worst Best Friend

One or Two Things I Learned About Love

Planet Janet

Sophie Pitt-Turnbull Discovers America

The Truth About My Success

Dyan Sheldon

CANDLEWICK PRESS

First U.S. edition 2018

Library of Congress Catalog Card Number pending
ISBN 978-0-7636-9354-1

17 18 19 20 21 22 BVG 10 9 8 7 6 5 4 3 2 1

Printed in Berryville, VA, U.S.A.

This book was typeset in Berkeley Oldstyle.

Candlewick Press
99 Dover Street
Somerville, Massachusetts 02144

visit us at www.candlewick.com

For the bluesmen, remembered and forgotten

Josh Is Reminded of a Song

The first time Josh sees her, a song he has heard only as background music pops into his head. The song is "I Saw Her Standing There." In fact, she isn't standing, she's sitting by the window in his language arts class, talking to Tilda Kopel, who is at the desk next to hers. She and Tilda seem to be friends, but Josh has never seen her before, so she must have moved to Parsons Falls over the summer. "I Saw Her Standing There." Of all the songs in all the world. He doesn't even like the Beatles—and he thinks it's a dumb song—but that's what he hears when he sees her. This is what he means about life being ironic; it gets you every time. Mercifully, his heart doesn't go *boom* the way it does in the lyrics. All it does is stumble a little. On this day, the start of a new school year, she is wearing an electric-blue top, green skinny jeans, and a gauzy silver scarf wound through her hair, some of which is pink. She smiles—not at him, at Tilda—and he feels as if he's been struck by lightning, only without being killed or permanently scarred. He stops so short at the sight of her that the boy behind walks into him. Only Mr. Burleigh's desk prevents Josh from falling flat on his face. Talk about making an entrance. Everyone notices him, though not, of course, in a way that is good. Especially since Mr. Burleigh notices him most of all.

"And who might you be?" Mr. Burleigh is known for his death-ray looks and scalpel-like sarcasm. That and his general irascibility.

Josh tells him.

"Josh Shine." Mr. Burleigh's eyebrows draw together like a bolt. "Your reputation precedes you, Mr. Shine. Much as rats preceded the plague."

He can only wonder which reputation. Would Mr. Burleigh have heard about his run-in with the head of the math department—when Josh, the department's star student, told Mr. Lattery his solution was wrong and got detention for insubordination, even though he was right? His petition for more vegetarian options than pizza in the lunchroom? The failed campaign he led last year to donate the money earmarked for the Christmas dance to the food bank? His considerable skill at chess?

Mr. Burleigh doesn't smile; he smirks. "Didn't you cause an explosion in the science lab last spring?"

"That was someone else." It was true that Josh had been there—and that he'd been marched through the school to the principal's office like a prisoner of war (minus the handcuffs and bag over his head)—but he'd been counting down, not blowing up. "And it was an accident."

The new girl by the window isn't the only one who laughs, but she is the only one whose laughter sounds the way hot fudge sauce tastes.

Embarrassed and possibly injured, Josh collapses into the nearest seat. She is pretty. Not stop-breathing gorgeous, but there's something about her. And he is definitely attracted. He has, however, no aspirations. This girl isn't in his league. The fact that she is already tight with Tilda Kopel—born to be Prom Queen if not Queen of the Universe—makes that pretty clear. Tilda Kopel doesn't hang out with the lower orders; she's not *in* the in crowd, she *is* the in crowd. If Josh fainted on the sidewalk in front of Tilda, she wouldn't step over him, she'd step on him. Possibly laughing. They've been in school together since first grade, but she's never given any indication that she can see him, unless he's done something to embarrass himself. In eighth grade they were put in the same group for a history project, and she never once spoke to him. Not even when she was asking a question she knew he would be the one to answer. Not even when he spoke to her. Josh has never asked anyone out, but, if he ever does, he won't pick a pal of Tilda Kopel's; he'll pick someone from the same species as him.

Fixations Not Fantasies

Her name is Jenevieve Capistrano — though, as she told Mr. Burleigh on that first morning with a melt-that-block-of-steel smile, her friends call her Jena.

At this particular moment, Josh, who is not her friend and has little chance of ever being one, is standing on a metal step stool at the bathroom sink, looking at himself in the mirror. Trying to see himself as Jenevieve Capistrano would see him — if she saw him, which seems unlikely. Since he's shorter than just about everyone else, when she does look his way her eyes probably go straight to the person behind him. He needs the stool so his chin isn't lost below the bottom of the glass.

He thinks about her a lot. Not constantly. He has more to occupy his mind than Jenevieve Capistrano. But often. As if she's stuck in his brain and can't get out. This happens to him all the time with songs. He hears a song for the first time and it's so good that he can't stop thinking about it. If he can, he'll sit down right away and start working out the music on his guitar. He'll fall asleep with it running through his head, and wake up with it still going. If he hears it playing, he'll stop to listen till it's over. When he was little he'd refuse to leave places if a song he liked was on the radio or the sound system. It drove his parents crazy. People were always asking what was wrong with that boy, standing in the doorway with his coat and hat on, rapt as if being spoken to by God. But that kind of thing has never happened with a girl. Not until now. No matter where he is—at school, in town, at home—part of him is looking out for her. *She might be around that corner. . . . She might step through that door. . . . She might be in that coffee shop having a cappuccino. . . .* He's like a smoke alarm waiting for the toast to burn. He'll be on his computer, or eating his supper, or hanging out with his friends and suddenly realize that he has no idea what's going on because he's thinking about Jenevieve Capistrano. *Where does she live? Does she like cats? Has she ever heard of Robert Johnson?*

The light over the sink is bright enough that he can see every mark, every scar, every bump, and every stray hair on his face, which does nothing to improve his appearance. Airbrushing would improve his appearance.

Or someone else's face. Nonetheless, he doesn't slouch, but raises his chin and sticks out his chest. He looks exactly as he always looks, only holding his breath so as not to fog the glass. "Get real, Shine," he advises himself. "What Jenevieve Capistrano would see if she ever looked at you is a geek." Not someone cool and desirable, but a short, skinny boy who wears wire-rimmed glasses and his hair longer than that of guys who aren't aspiring blues musicians. His mother says he has an interesting face, which translated into non-mother-speak means that though he isn't exactly ugly, he's kind of funny-looking. Misshapen ears. Bump in his nose. Caterpillar eyebrows trying to crawl toward each other to meet. More a dinghy than a dreamboat.

He sticks his tongue out at himself. What's wrong with him, obsessing about a girl he doesn't even know? Because that's what he's doing: he's obsessing. Fixating. He's not fantasizing, thank God—not imagining her appearing in his room naked or anything like that. He doesn't even imagine kissing her. He just can't stop thinking about her, that's all. And he's wrong, it's not like the first time he heard a song he loved and went around singing it under his breath for a week. It's more like last Christmas when he heard that dumb chipmunk song on the radio and it stayed with him till New Year's. Do they even make Hula-Hoops anymore?

"You know what?" he says in a tough-guy voice, looking himself in the eyes as well as he can through two layers of glass. "You're as stupid as a Ravenous Bugblatter Beast of Traal."

According to *The Hitchhiker's Guide to the Galaxy*, one of Josh's favorite books, the Ravenous Bugblatter Beasts of Traal are the most stupid creatures in the universe. Josh stares at the mirror, thinking about Jena Capistrano. It's possible that he's stupider.

"This isn't your brain making you act like this," Josh tells his reflection, "it's your age." Hormones. Apart from what he knows about human development from advanced biology, he has surreptitiously read up on adolescence in his mother's magazines. Unlike your average textbook, the magazines give a lot of useful anecdotal information about teenagers and how they behave and why. Unfortunately, this didn't offer him as much consolation or hope as he would have liked. It's good to know that other people suffer in the same way, but it doesn't make him suffer less. It doesn't make anything any better or more bearable. Indeed, if the biologists and advice columnists of the nation are to be believed, there isn't anything that would. Hormones are a force unto themselves. They're like the barbarian hordes that sacked Rome; they just take over and trample everything in their path. Josh was counting on a growth spurt during puberty—possibly accompanied by muscles, broad shoulders, and a voice like B. B. King's—which was what the magazines said could happen, but all he got was acne, hair, and, it seems, mental instability.

"It's not even like she's really that special." He gives himself an ironic smile. "I mean, she's cute—and she seems pretty smart and nice and everything, but so is Charley Patton." And Charley Patton, being a cat, can jump from the floor to Josh's shoulder, which isn't a talent likely to be shared by Jenevieve Capistrano. Josh sighs. Still staring at himself, he starts talking to Jenevieve Capistrano. "Looking at it rationally, it's actually inexplicable. No offense, but you are just another girl on a planet full of girls. And let's be honest here. There's a very strong probability that I wouldn't like you if I actually got to know you. You are really pally with Tilda Kopel, and she and I aren't exactly twin souls." If Tilda has a twin soul it's probably in Hell. "All I ever hear Tilda talk about are clothes and makeup and stuff like that. She's a gossip. And she's really full of herself. You'd think every other girl who ever lived was just God practicing to make her." There's a knock on the bathroom door that Josh doesn't hear. "For all I know, you're probably so boring you could put a whole football team to sleep in the middle of a game. And so what if you're cute?" He doesn't hear the doorknob rattle, either, or his mother call his name with a certain amount of concern. "Lots of girls are cute. There must be millions of girls in the world who are cute, and the odds are that the majority of them are cuter than you. Way cuter. Besides, being cute doesn't make you a good person. For all I know you're not half as nice as you seem. You're just cute and you have a great smile because you take good care of your tee—"

"Josh? Josh?" Now his mother is banging on the door. Urgently. "Josh! Who are you talking to in there?"

A girl I don't know, who isn't here. Who else?

"No one, Mom. I was just practicing a speech for school."

"Oh. A speech." She sounds relieved. She was probably figuring that on top of tragically losing his father at such a young age, her only child was now losing his mind. "I was getting a little worried. You've been in there quite a while."

"I was just coming out." With one last look in the mirror, he steps off the stool—and lands on Charley Patton, who was resting behind him. Charley Patton howls. It's the kind of howl that once echoed through dense, primordial forests on dark, Neanderthal nights. Josh jumps into the air and crashes into the shelf where his mother keeps her makeup.

"Josh? Josh! What happened? What's going on in there? Are you all right?"

He picks up a handful of tubes and jars.

From behind the toilet bowl, Charley hisses.

"I'm terrific," says Josh.

It has to be some kind of miracle that so many people actually survive adolescence.

Josh's New Year's Resolutions Never Last Long, Either

Josh is resolved. Determined as a superhero sworn to rid the city of crime and evil mischief. He can't go on like this; he is going to banish Jenevieve Capistrano from his mind. She is just another attractive girl; just another cute grain of sand on a very large beach. It is in this mood that he strides into school like a captain boarding his ship. *I am in command.*

Captain Shine's command lasts less than a minute. She is standing in the main foyer, talking to some girls who aren't Tilda Kopel but could be if Tilda left town. She's not just another pretty face; she stands out like a diamond in a bag of marbles.

She smiles. As always, it isn't at him; as always, it makes him think that the world might be a better place than he knows it is. Josh comes to a dead stop. It may be that the girls are all about to go their separate ways. If they do, if Jenevieve, on her own, walks past him, then he might have a chance to say something to her. If he were taller and belonged to the right group and looked more like a movie star than a near-sighted bush baby, he could simply walk up to her and welcome her to Parsons Falls. *Hi, you're new here. Let me know if you need someone to show you around.* But he isn't and he doesn't, so he needs some vague but viable excuse in order to approach her. A question about their language arts homework. A comment about Mr. Burleigh. A *Hey, did you drop this pen?* Anything to get the ball rolling. Part of him makes a pained face and groans. So far his attempts to roll the ball have all ended up in the gutter.

The first time he got up the nerve to speak to her he was making his way to history and she was strolling down the hall with Tilda and another Miss Wonderful Teenager with teeth like hospital tiles and the confidence of a megalomaniac. Tilda was talking (she's always talking; odds are she talked in the womb). Josh's stomach clenched and his heart impersonated a hammer, but he forced himself to look at Jena and give her his best this-is-a-friendly-town smile. She was looking straight ahead, in his direction, but she didn't smile back. As they passed he said, "Hi." Not loudly. He was so afraid of shouting or squeaking with nerves that it came out as no more than a whisper. She didn't hear him. Or if she did hear some unintelligible mumble she decided to ignore it. *Don't encourage the masses.*

The second time, as in his daydreams (and many movies), he turned a corner and practically walked into her. She was leaning against a locker, looking bored. Her evil twin was nowhere in sight, so he guessed that it was Tilda's locker and Jenevieve was waiting for her. He was so surprised to catch her alone that he didn't think. He just stopped in front of her and blurted out, "I guess you must get a lot of bird jokes, huh?" She blinked, surprised or possibly startled—as if she hadn't known he could talk. And then she smiled the way you would if a crazy person came up to you in the street and said he was from Alpha Centauri and needed five dollars to get home. "Bird jokes? I don't know what you mean." And who could blame her? What's wrong with him? No, really—what is wrong with him? You just don't walk up to someone you've never spoken to and start babbling about some obscure song that last charted in the 1950s. He might as well have asked her what time it was in Burkina Faso. He definitely wasn't going to explain about the swallows returning to Capistrano. He couldn't. He was struck dumb with embarrassment. Mumbling, "Sorry," and never meaning it more, he turned so quickly that the only reason he didn't plow into anybody was because he walked straight into the bank of lockers.

After that fiasco, he would have had trouble shouting "Fire!" if he'd seen flames rising behind her. The only words he's said directly to Jena since those first two botched attempts were "Hey, I'm sorry." Three times. The first when he somehow managed to step on her; then when he knocked her books out of her arms; and finally when he bent down suddenly to pick up his pen and she practically fell over him. He may kill her long before he gets to speak to her.

He'd like to write a song about her, get her out of his system that way. Unfortunately, there isn't much that rhymes with Jenevieve. *Give me leave . . . No reprieve . . . Wipe your nose upon my sleeve.* And even less that rhymes with Jena. *I'm gonna penna song to Jena.* Christ. Next time he gets fixated on someone he's going to take his lead from Huddie Ledbetter and make it someone with a name like Irene.

Now He Knows Why It's Called a Bull Session

It's a Saturday night. Most Saturday nights Josh hangs out with Carver and Sal at one of their homes to watch obscure movies or play games. Carver Jefferson and Armando "Sal" Salcedo are two of his closest friends. Carver lives in the house behind Josh's, and they've been inseparable for as long as either can remember. They met Sal in middle school and immediately became three. Carver is the scientist, Josh the musician, and Sal the next Wes Anderson or, possibly, Martin Scorsese. Each is something of a misfit in school, but they suit each other well. In eighth grade there was a discussion in Mr. Juniper's science class about the possibility of life on other planets and, if there were life, was it possible that extraterrestrials ever visited the earth. In this discussion Sal, Carver, and Josh—possibly influenced by their love of *Star Trek*—all said yes, and the rest of the class said no. "We're like the Three Musketeers," said Sal. "More like the Three Mouseketeers," said Josh. Everyone else called them the Pod Squad—though, mercifully, few people remember that now.

The movie has ended. Tonight they watched a science-fiction film about highly evolved aliens who come to save the earth from the destruction caused by humans, which has led to a discussion about entertainment versus information.

Right now would be a good example of how Josh's preoccupation with Jenevieve "My Friends Call Me Jena" Capistrano interferes with his everyday existence. He sits in an armchair facing Carver and Sal, looking as if he is following their argument with thoughtful interest, but, having changed his mind about Jenevieve Capistrano being another girl among millions, what he's really doing is wondering if he'll ever get to talk to her in a meaningful and unembarrassing way. The way he talks to his family, his friends, and his cat.

"But it was informative," Sal is saying. "It showed you what human nature is like. I mean, come on, man, look what happened to the poor aliens. All they wanted to do was help. But we wouldn't let them. That was the whole point of the movie."

"I get all that," concedes Carver. "I'm not debating

it had a message, but it was buried in shoot-outs and chases."

Sal's sigh is heavy with sarcasm. They have had this discussion — or one very similar — before. "But—"

"But, firstly, most people who see that movie aren't going to come away musing about human behavior or how we're killing the planet. They're going to be thinking about what they'd do if there was an alien invasion. They're going to be wondering if they could make a bunker in the basement."

"And secondly?"

"And secondly, even if they are thinking, 'Boy, people are pretty grim, what advanced life-form would want to try to help us when, if we don't kill them, we'd put them in a zoo?' they're going to forget that by the time they get in the car. What they'll remember is whether or not it was exciting and had some good jokes."

"So what's wrong with that?" demands Sal. "Everything doesn't have to be a documentary about the end of life as we know it." Carver is going to be an environmental scientist; when it's his turn to pick a movie they almost always wind up watching a documentary. A depressing documentary, according to some. "You can entertain and inform at the same time. People don't want lectures."

"No, what they want are special effects. Talking toys.

Flying broomsticks. Animals that sing and dance. So they can forget about anything serious and just have a good time."

"*¡Madre de dios!*" Sal's voice rises. "As usual, you're totally ignoring the power of plot and character."

Carver's voice doesn't rise; he might be talking about socks. "And, as usual, you are totally ignoring the talent people have for putting their heads in the sand and seeing only what they want to see."

Carver's calm only makes Sal more emotional. He waves his hands in the air. "That's why you wrap your message in a good story. Lure them into it. Sugarcoating on the pill."

"Now's not the time for that shit," says Carver. "This planet has some serious problems that need some serious solutions."

"But you love *Star Trek* and *Blade Runner* and *Hitchhiker's Guide*—"

"They haven't changed anything, though, have they? They've entertained and amused and made some people a lot of money."

"Josh, man," moans Sal, "help me out here, will you? I'm starting to lose the will to live." Josh continues staring into space. Sal picks up a pretzel from the bowl on the table and aims it at Josh's head. It bounces off his glasses.

"Hey!" He blinks like someone who's just stepped out of a deep, dark cave. "What's up with you? What'd you do that for?"

"What's up with *me*?" Sal laughs. Sarcastically. "What's up with *you*? You've been acting like a refugee from *The Boy Who Wasn't There* all week." *The Boy Who Wasn't There* is a favorite movie of Sal's, about a teenager whose body is taken over by beings who can move through time the way humans cross a room.

"Nothing's up with me." Josh picks the pretzel from his lap and pops it into his mouth. "I was just thinking, that's all."

"You know, Sal's right," says Carver. "You have definitely been mind-surfing all week. Either that or looking around like you're expecting the cops to turn up."

"I'm not the one who has to worry about the cops, Jefferson." It was Carver who almost blew up the science lab last year. He was conducting an experiment to prove the inaccuracy of drones—which was the other thing it accomplished.

"So, if not the police, who is it you've been looking for?" asks Sal.

"No one. You're imagining things. My eyes probably wander because I'm tired of staring at your ugly mugs."

"I bet I know what's on your mind," says Sal. "It's a

girl, isn't it? It has to be." How does the boy whose own mind is always occupied with scripts and camera angles know that? "You've had that lobotomized look lately."

"I wasn't thinking about a girl," lies Josh.

But apparently not convincingly. Carver shakes his head. Thoughtfully considering. "Oh no, I do believe Sal is onto something here." He eyes Josh as if he's a piece of scientific evidence. "Now that he's mentioned it, I've noticed it, too. He's right, isn't he? You're all warped out by a girl."

"No, I'm not." But because he's so caught by surprise, he decides to reshape the lie. "To tell you the truth, I was thinking about girls—but in a general kind of way."

"In a general kind of way?" repeats Carver. "Like you only just noticed them? What were you wondering—how they got here?"

"Just in general, Carver. You know, like you might think about the ocean or the Arctic Circle or whatever. We don't talk much about girls and stuff like that."

"Nor do we talk much about rappelling or hunting," says Carver. "But that's because we're not exactly involved in those things, either."

"Yeah, but unlike hanging off a mountain or shooting deer, we will be involved with girls. Someday. Won't we?" As unlikely as it sometimes seems, there is a strong probability that, eventually, at least one of them will have a date.

"So you want an old-fashioned bull session, is that what you want?" laughs Sal. "Like on the Memorable Fourth?"

The Memorable Fourth of July occurred two summers ago when the whole Salcedo clan gathered for a holiday barbecue. Because beds were needed, Sal was moved to a tent in the backyard. He liberated a couple of unclaimed six-packs, and Carver and Josh crashed there with him. There was a lot of talk about girls and stuff like that, that night. Though how memorable any of it was is up for debate. What they remember most is waking up in terror when the raccoons knocked over the garbage cans, and then managing to collapse the tent in their panic.

"I guess. Yeah. Something like that." But sober. "It's just that I don't think I even know how to get started with a girl."

Carver grins. "Oh, I think we all know how to get started, Josh. You didn't miss Sex Ed 101."

"I don't mean sex. I mean dating. You guys know how dating works? You read the manual?"

"Don't quote me or anything"—Carver is good at sardonically smug—"but I believe you begin by asking someone out. And then you go out. It's an A, B, C kind of thing." Unable to resist, he adds, "Like sex."

"But what if you're, you know, not so sure about asking her out in the first place?"

"Not sure you want to, or not sure you should?" asks Sal.

"You know you want to. That's the part you're sure of."

Sal absentmindedly picks up a pretzel. "You mean you're infatuated? Is that what you mean?" Still not looking at it, he breaks the pretzel in half. "It's not just that you think it's time to go on a date. You have a thing for somebody."

"Ah, an infatuation . . ." Carver makes it sound like an exotic but deadly disease. "Statistically, I suppose it's bound to happen to one of us eventually. Like cancer or going bald."

"*Dios mío,* man, you don't have to be so negative." Sal snaps the pretzel again. "They're not the same thing at all. What's so bad about having a crush on someone? I think it's cool."

"Maybe." Carver sounds as far from convinced as Earth is from Mars. "But, if you ask me, it can distract you from what you should be concentrating on."

Sal groans. "Man, you really are a young fogey, Carver. You must've been born middle-aged. No wonder you're already thinking about going bald." Now in crumbs and pieces, the pretzel falls to the floor, but Sal doesn't notice. He leans toward Carver. "If you ask me, it's a lot more normal to have the hots for someone than it is to act like you're some kind of monk and above all that stuff."

"I'm not acting like anything," says Carver. "I'm just saying that I've decided not to even think about getting involved with anyone until I've at least done my master's. Get the important things out of the way first."

"Yeah, right," says Sal. "Who are you kidding? You know damn well that high-school girls aren't turned on by guys who talk about nothing but greenhouse gases. You have less chance of getting a date than of stopping climate change."

"Women can be very distracting," says Carver. Environmental science is no place for someone who isn't stubborn. "You have to get your priorities right."

"What about your biological imperatives?" demands Sal. "You going to put them on hold till you get your master's? *Hang on, millions of years of evolution, I just have to get accepted to a PhD program and then we'll be good to go.*"

"There are ways of dealing with biological imperatives." Carver winks. "As I'm pretty sure you know."

"Excuse me," interrupts Josh. He is not the first person in mankind's history to wish he'd never said anything. Maybe he's the one who should be a monk, in an order that takes a vow of silence. "You don't mind if I rejoin the conversation, do you? I mean, you forgot that I wasn't talking about sex. Or infatuation, or feelings. All I said was, what if you're not sure about asking someone out? None of what you've been yakking about has anything to do with where we started." At least now he knows what the "bull" in *bull session* refers to, and it isn't the chromosome makeup of the people having it. "Would you ask her out if you didn't think she was guaranteed to say yes? That's all I was wondering."

"Yes," says Sal. "Absolutely. If you think there's a chance."

"But that's just the point. You don't know if there's a chance. She could laugh in your face. Or tweet to all her friends and have half the school laughing at you in a matter of minutes. What then?"

Sal obviously hadn't thought of any of that. He's silent for a few seconds, imagining a moment decades from now when he steps up to collect his Best Director award and the presenter says, *Aren't you the Armando Salcedo who made a fool of himself in high school by asking out the wrong girl?* "Oh, man, it's tricky, isn't it?" He shakes his head. “But I still think it’s better to say something, not take it to your grave with you.”

“I disagree,” says Carver. “No way. Unless you’re at least ninety-eight percent sure she’d think it was a good idea. Or not the worst idea she’s ever heard in her life.”

So now we know why Carver has so many principles, thinks Josh. *He’s afraid of being rejected, too.*

Josh Manages to Go Almost the Entire Morning without Thinking of Jenevieve Capistrano

Josh's other closest friend is Ramona Minamoto. Sal recently asked him if he was interested in Ramona, and it was such an unexpected question that Josh had to ask for clarification. "You mean as a girl?"

"No, as a chess partner." Sal sighed dramatically. "Yes, as a girl. I don't see why you're acting so surprised. She is a girl. And you are pretty tight with her." He fidgeted with the silver bracelet he always wears. "You spend a lot of time together."

"Have you and I ever met?" asked Josh. "Christ, you know Mo and I are just friends. She's like my sister."

Sal said Josh wouldn't say that if he actually had a sister. "Carver has it the worst," judged Sal. "He has three of them. But, believe me, one's plenty. She never lets up." Always shouting, bickering, criticizing, nagging, and blaming. She once even yelled at him because it was raining. "Tell you one thing, I wouldn't want to be on trial and have her on the jury, because, guaranteed, she'd recommend hanging."

But Josh has known Ramona almost as long as he's known Carver. Their mothers are best friends, so they've pretty much grown up together. Family vacations. Shared babysitters and sleepovers when they were little. He's almost as close to her as he is to Carver. It was Ramona who rescued him by shouting "Bruno! Stop!" when the Polos' boxer chased him onto the roof of their SUV—and Bruno, who up until that second could easily have been mistaken for the Hound of the Baskervilles, stopped. Ramona had to help Josh down. Which was only slightly less embarrassing than the afternoon he sprained his ankle and she carried him home. She was also there the time he ill-advisedly tried to give Charley Patton a bath, and he was there the time she hennaed her hair and her head swelled up. She's practically one of the guys—the breasts and the six earrings notwithstanding.

Today is Sunday. On Sunday mornings Josh and Ramona go to yoga together. Josh has been playing both chess and the guitar since he was five; his mother thought it was time he took up an activity where he moves more than his fingers. Carver climbs and kayaks (brawn as well as brains), and Sal runs and plays golf (because that's what movie people do). Josh, however, isn't interested in any activity in which he might drown, be hit by a car, be bored to death, or break something, especially his hands. When he was younger he was clumsy and had so many broken bones and black eyes that his doctor asked him what extreme sport he did. Josh said, "Walking." It was Ramona who suggested her yoga class. Core strength and spiritual depth—what could be wrong with that?

"Not only is it indoors and the chance of injury fairly minimal," said Ramona, "but you'll like it. Plus, super bonus, you'll be the only male." She gave him a wise-guy grin. "Give you a chance to see what it's like to be really popular with women." What a sense of humor.

Two of Ramona's promises turned out to be untrue: in the summer they often hold the class in the garden (where he seems to be allergic to the grass), and he isn't the only one who has hurt himself doing an asana (although he is the only one who lost his balance in *kakasana* and bit his own tongue).

And two have turned out to be true: he does like it, and he is the sole male. The token male. Ramona's the only other person his age, but he still enjoys being surrounded by women who like him and aren't his mother. It does make a nice change.

Today the added benefit of the class was that he was

concentrating so hard on demonstrating partner poses with Ramona—an example of two sets of hands and feet not making things easier—that he didn't think of Jenevieve Capistrano even once.

And he isn't thinking of her now as he and Ramona leave the studio together. She lopes beside him, almost as tall as an NBA player, her long hair streaming behind her. Josh is nearly trotting to keep up.

"Oh God, that is so funny!" gasps Ramona. "Trust Burleigh to remember you were involved in the science explosion."

He's been catching her up on some of the major events of his week. Though not all of them.

"I can already tell it's not going to be a good year," says Josh. "He calls everybody else by their first names, but me he calls Mr. Shine."

She glances over at him. "Why? What else did you do?"

"Nothing much." This is what he means about her being like a sister: she knows him really well. "We did kind of have some words."

"Oh God, Josh. School just started." This is another thing that makes her like a sister: she's always quick to get on his case. "What kind of words?"

"You know . . ."

Ramona rolls her eyes. Oh, yes, she knows.

The first difference of opinion was when Josh wanted to read a novel not on the course list for the term (Mr. Burleigh's sardonic response caused general hilarity). The second was when Josh challenged one of Mr. Burleigh's handed-down-from-heaven-on-a-stone-tablet rules of grammar and proved him wrong (nobody laughed at that, least of all Jake Burleigh).

"It's your own fault," says Ramona as they cross the street for their after-class tea at the Laughing Moon Café. "What is it with you and authority? You never know when to keep your mouth shut."

"Don't start, Mo. You know if you'd been there you'd've been on my side."

"But I like to save my ammunition for major battles. I wouldn't've made a federal case out of something like that."

"Okay, I admit I was pushing it wanting to pick my own book, even if it was thematically in line with what we're doing." The truth is that Mr. Burleigh irritates Josh as much as Josh irritates him. He could only be more supercilious if he were twins. "But with the grammar thing, he was totally in the wrong."

"Oh, please. . . . Seriously, Josh? You corrected Mr. Burleigh in front of the whole class? Your common sense must still be on vacation."

"But he was wrong, Mo. He's supposed to be giving us an education, not dictation."

"This is Burleigh we're talking about, Josh, not Socrates." The philosopher Socrates believed in asking questions of his students; the high-school teacher Jake Burleigh believes in providing the answers and having his students repeat them.

"I can't help it. I have a highly developed sense of right and wrong."

Ramona laughs. Possibly at him, not with him. "Yeah. Like at the sanctuary that time." Their class had an outing to a bird refuge. The birds were all raptors—hawks and falcons, eagles and owls—and though most of them were in large cages, some were displayed on outdoor perches to which they were tethered, and made to do tricks. Josh thought this was cruel, and exploitative—as if they were toys. He made quite a scene.

"Oh, come on, Mo. That was in second grade!"

"They almost threw us out!"

"But it wasn't fair the way they treated the birds. Somebody had to say something."

"Have you noticed that it's always you?" The bird sanctuary wasn't the last time something like that happened. "I swear, I've lost count of how many places we've been asked to leave because you couldn't keep your mouth shut." Her hair brushes his face as she shakes her head. "You wouldn't last ten minutes in any self-respecting dictatorship. Somebody like Kim Jong-un would have you for breakfast." She yanks open the door and waves him through. "Which I guess is one of the things I . . . like about you."

They get their teas and go to their usual table in the corner — neither of them likes to sit in the window like a mannequin. Ramona puts her cup down and plunks herself into an armchair. Josh takes the seat across from her.

"Wow, that was a great class, wasn't it?!" Ramona stretches her legs under the table, accidentally kicking his foot. "I really feel energized."

"I'm glad you feel energized," says Josh. "I wasn't sure I'd make it across the street. That double downward dog nearly cut my young life tragically short." Her feet placed not on the ground but on his back. He was terrified he was going to bring them both crashing to the floor. In which case she'd probably crush him — or at least crack a couple of ribs.

"Oh, please. . . . It was great and you know it." She kicks him again, this time intentionally. "You're a walking contradiction, you know that, Shine? You'd correct God if you thought He'd made a mistake or something. But you always think you can't do things you can do — usually really well. I don't know why you're like that."

"I lack confidence and have a poor self-image when it comes to anything physical. Except playing the guitar." He carefully scoops the teabag from his cup and squeezes it against the spoon. "I thought you'd know that by now."

"Oh, I know it." Ramona pulls her bag out by the string and chucks it at the side of the saucer. "I just try to ignore it." She takes a packet of brown sugar from the bowl on the table. "Anyway, everybody else was really impressed even if you weren't. I can't wait to see Mayana's pictures."

Mayana is their teacher. She changed her name from Mary when she got the yin-yang tattoo on her ankle and the crescent moon stud in her nose.

"I can. I'm not really at my most photogenic when I have you balancing on me."

"You're too modest." She shakes the sugar into her cup, scattering grains over the table. "Mostly all anyone's going to see is the back of your head, and that is your best side." She stirs her tea. "Anyway, I'm really glad we have the yoga even if you think it is life-threatening. I've hardly seen you since school started. Not to talk to for more than a couple of minutes. We don't even have the same lunch period. Yoga's all we have left."

"Our loss is the post-postmodernists' gain." Ramona's other friends and lunchtime companions are artistic types, all eccentric clothes and personally decorated portfolios.

"Not so. I still have Zara to eat with, but the rest of them have been shoved around by the bureaucratic powers, too." She's still stirring. "I miss you." If she doesn't stop stirring she'll put a hole in the bottom of the cup. "Zara never gripes about meat-eaters and she's crap at Name That Tune." Two activities at which Josh excels. "And even if you and I didn't always eat together, at least we saw each other every day and had a chance to do more than wave across a corridor."

Josh takes a sip of his tea. "I didn't know you cared."

Ramona's spoon falls to the table; her laugh jumps. "Don't worry, Shine, I don't care. It's more like missing a headache. I guess I got used to hanging with you in the summer." He's wondering if he's tasting licorice or fennel and doesn't respond. "You know," she persists, "when we went up to the lake?"

Her tone makes him look up. "For Christ's sake, Mo, it's only September. Did you think I forgot already?"

She picks up her cup, tea sloshing over the side. "Well, you didn't say anything."

"Sorry. I got distracted for a second. Of course

I remember the summer. This'll amaze you, but it almost feels like yesterday." Carver was away protecting some trees, Sal was taking a film course, and Josh's band had broken up for the summer, so he got talked into spending a couple of weeks at the Minamotos' cabin in the Adirondacks. Summer is a busy time in the world of botanical medicine, and Mr. Minamoto was away, too. As Josh's mother put it, it was "Just us girls." Just us girls and Josh.

This time Ramona's laugh rattles more than leaps. "But it was fun, wasn't it?"

That depends on your concept of fun. Chopping wood (at which he's useless), being bitten by insects (for which he has a natural aptitude), and lying awake at night listening to the thumpings, rustlings, and howlings (certain that every wildcat and coyote in the state was trying to get in).

"Yeah, it was good." It wasn't the blues festival that he would have preferred, but it was a lot better than he'd been afraid it would be. Josh's pioneer spirit is easily satisfied with a chorus of "Old Dan Tucker," but Hannah Shine and Jade Minamoto like to wallow in nature. They hike, they paddle, they hunt for edible plants. His fear was that he'd be force-marched through the woods or strapped into a raft and shoved downriver — two activities with the potential to end really badly. He would either get lost and starve to death before the rescuers found him, be attacked by a bear and have to be identified by his teeth, or simply drown. Josh knows an appropriate song for each of those scenarios, but of course he'd have been dead and in no position to play them.

Ramona stops smiling. She looks at her cup as if it's let her down. "You didn't enjoy it?" Ramona more than enjoyed it. If she has any complaints about the vacation it was that it could have been longer. Which is because the only fault she can find with Josh is that he makes her look even taller than she is (though this isn't something she holds against him). "I thought you did." If Ramona were the weather it would be overcast with the possibility of showers. "I thought we had a really good time."

Damn, now he's hurt her feelings.

"I didn't mean I didn't have a good time, Mo. Of course I did. It was great." Which actually is true. More true than he would have believed possible. Fortunately for his health and safety, it rained a lot, so the hikes through tick- and poison ivy–infested woods and the rides on raging rivers were limited. He and Ramona were left to their own devices while the mothers visited every antique store, junk shop, and barn sale in a hundred-mile radius. Josh and Ramona's own devices were playing board games and music. Ramona is easy to hang out with, and not only plays a decent game of chess but is unbelievably good at Risk for a girl who once wore peace-symbol earrings. "It was cool watching you achieve world domination. But the best was the jamming." He'd heard her play before, of course—she's been in one orchestra or another since elementary school—but it was always at concerts, formal as tuxedos. He'd never played with her or realized what a mean fiddler a girl who trained as a classical violinist could be.

The clouds pass and the smile reappears on Ramona's face. "Me, too. It was totally chill." She pauses as if choosing her words—as if she has something important to say—but what she says is, "So how are you doing now that we're back in the real world? Everything good?"

"I'm okay. Busy. Not much time for bowling or ice hockey, but we all have to make sacrifices. It's a big year for the chess club. And there's the band, of course. We want to try and get some gigs this year. We're already booked for the garden in the spring."

"Madison Square?"

"Jerym Jefferson's." It's Carver's father's birthday in May and he's willing to have them play at his party if he gets to sit in on the kazoo. "So if you're interested in joining us we could use an ace fiddle player."

"Really?" Her voice sounds like a yes, but her face looks like a no.

"Yeah, really. It would be phenomenal to have you in the band."

"Geez, I wish you'd asked me sooner. I'd love to play with you. But I'm pretty busy right now, too. You know I joined the drama club."

"I do?"

He wonders if his mother taught her to sigh like that.

"Didn't Sal tell you?"

"Sal?" When did she see Sal without Josh?

"You guys . . . It's amazing that men invented telecommunications when you find it so hard to pass along basic information." She sighs again. "Yes, Josh, I'm in the drama club. Mr. Boxhill, you know he's the advisor? And he directs all the plays?" Josh nods. He knows it now. "Anyway, Mr. Boxhill asked me if I'd be in charge of the costumes for this year's play. They're doing *Bye Bye Birdie*."

"*Bye Bye Birdie?* Isn't that a musical?" He thinks of Ramona as more an Ibsen or Arthur Miller kind of girl.

"That's right." She bobs her head back and forth. "There are a lot of peppy songs and dancing." She laughs. "It's not my choice, obviously. If it were up to me, we'd be doing *Sweeney Todd* or *West Side Story*. But I said yes before I knew what they'd picked. He just stopped me in the hall and asked me if I'd take the job. Said he's always noticed my clothes."

Of course Boxhill's noticed her clothes; he'd have to be either blind or living halfway across the world not to. Everybody notices Ramona's clothes. What she doesn't find in thrift and vintage stores, she designs and makes herself. Today, for example, she's wearing leggings, a short skirt, and a long-sleeved T-shirt with a tunic over it. The leggings, skirt, and tunic are in different patterns and colors; the T-shirt, in yet two more colors, is striped.

"So anyway," Ramona continues, "I'm going to be pretty involved with that for a while. Zara's going to help me with the shopping. You know, because unlike some people she doesn't have a phobia about it."

Some people being Josh. "It's not a phobia, Mo. It's just a gut-wrenching fear."

She makes a *whatever* face. "Well, anyway, even with Zara's help it's going to be crazy for a while."

Possibly because of the shopping-phobia crack he says, "I still can't believe you're working on *Bye Bye Birdie*. Isn't it kind of hokey?"

"Not everybody thinks so." Though Ramona isn't one of them. "And at least they're making some changes. Sal's idea is we should set it in the late sixties, early seventies. Put more of an edge on it. Which I would really like. You can get pretty wild with clothes in the sixties, but the fifties? It's all ponytails and poodle skirts and squeaky clean. So I'm really glad he signed on for assistant director, even though it was a massive surprise. I mean, Sal? Who'da thunk, right?"

Josh got a little lost among the ponytails and poodle skirts but now he says, "Sal's assistant director?" Why would Armando Salcedo suddenly join the drama club? He doesn't want to act. He doesn't need another extracurricular activity to look good on his college applications. He's always saying what lousy films plays usually make.

"Oh, you have to be kidding." Her eyes widen. "You mean he didn't tell you that either?"

"No. He did. I'm pretty sure he did." Josh has a vague memory of Sal saying something last night, but it must have been when Josh wasn't really paying close attention. "No, he definitely did."

"Well, I don't know about you, but I was pretty amazed," says Ramona. "I thought he was a total cinephile. Hardcore. Remember that movie he made in eighth grade instead of writing a book report?"

As if he could forget. Josh was the only one who wore glasses, so he was forced to play Harry Potter.

Ramona's laugh isn't the hot-fudge-sauce ripple that

Jenevieve Capistrano's is but more like a needle-scratching-a-vinyl-record cackle. "I swear, I can still see Mrs. Gillespie's face when he handed her the disc. She didn't know whether to laugh or cry."

What Josh remembers is tripping over his wizard's robe (Jade Minamoto's black kimono) and falling into the Salcedos' pool.

"So what made Sal do it?" asks Ramona. "He can't've given up his obsession with the movies. I would've noticed if the earth stood still."

"I don't know." Josh shrugs. "I think he said something about a play being just like a movie but without car chases and tracking shots." And in this case with singing.

"Jesus." If she were a cartoon her caption would be: *Ramona is exasperated*. "That's it? You know, if you guys are communicating telepathically, it isn't working."

"That's all I remember."

She's definitely sighing more than usual today. "Well, I think it's way weird," says Ramona. "It's so out of character. But I have to admit, it's also nice to see a friendly face. Tell you the truth, I'm already finding it a little stressful."

"But it's what you want to do." Not fashion, of course, not Ramona Minamoto, the girl who believes that fashion is fascism. Ramona wants to be a costume designer.

"Yeah, I know. But it's kind of a nightmare and a dream come true at the same time, you know? It's a big challenge. I've only ever dressed myself before." She makes a here-comes-the-bad-news face. "It's not just that, though. The club isn't exactly a tranquil and meditative scene. There are a lot of drama queens flouncing around. I mean, you know who else is in the club. Of course."

He has no idea. "Is this a trick question?"

"Oh, Josh. You do too know. She's starred in every play since elementary school. She's the biggest prima donna of them all. If egos generated electricity she could solve the energy crisis all by herself."

"Oh, shit. Are we talking Tilda Kopel here?"

"Duh! Who else could it be?"

No one. The fact that he didn't think of her right away is proof that hormones are eating away his brain.

"You know you're not the only one who has an ugly past with her. I never got along with her. Not since elementary school when she told everybody I had head lice. Now just the sound of her voice sucks the joy right out of my heart. She's always so bouncy and bubbly—unless she's criticizing someone—she's like human Alka-Seltzer. Only on a nuclear scale. And remember that big fight we had a couple of years ago . . ."

Ramona launches into a detailed account of her most

recent historic fight with Tilda Kopel and the events leading up to it. Normally, Josh would find this story tears-in-your-eyes funny, but today — although he's looking right at her and he nods and smiles as needed — he isn't giving her his full attention. Although he hasn't given Jenevieve Capistrano a thought all morning, the mention of Tilda Kopel has put Jena back in his head. His mind starts formulating what is almost a geometric proof. Tilda Kopel and Jena are friends. Friends do things together. If Tilda Kopel is in the drama club, then Jena may join, too. If Jena joins the drama club, she and Ramona will get to know each other. If Jena and Ramona get to know each other, then they may become friends. Which would exponentially increase Josh's chances of meeting Jena and becoming friends with her as well.

As postulations go it might not be probable, but it is possible. He can get to know her and break the spell. Instead of imagining what she's like, he'll know what she's like. She won't be special because she's a new girl with some pink in her hair; she'll be just like all the girls he's been at school with forever and never looked at twice. There will be things wrong with her; things he doesn't like. He'll find out that not only has she never heard of Robert Johnson but also that the only music she listens to is *radio-put-me-in-a-coma-lalala*. And then he has an image of the two girls together and instantly realizes how ridiculous that is. Ramona Minamoto and Jenevieve Capistrano are not going to become friends. Not on this planet, and not in this lifetime. For God's sake, Jena's a normal teenage girl, and Ramona's Ramona. There's more chance of finding a yeti in your backyard than there is that the two of them will ever share a bag of potato chips, let alone a secret.

A shadow falls over him, as if the lights really have gone out, and Josh looks up. Ramona is on her feet.

"My God, will you look at the time," she's saying. "I have to skedaddle. So you'll do that for me, okay?"

"Do it?" Obviously, not everything she was talking about happened in ninth grade.

Ramona groans. "Oh God, Josh. You weren't listening to a word I said, were you? You're just like my dad."

He is nothing like her father. Frank Minamoto wears a necklace and clogs (unless it's snowing) and plays the zither.

"I guess I lost track for a minute."

She sighs. "Yeah, right."

"So what is it you want me to do?"

"It's no big deal." He can tell that her smile is supposed to reassure him. Which, naturally, makes him wary. It's going to be something he won't want to do. "Just take my yoga stuff to the gallery because I'm babysitting all afternoon and I don't want to lug it with me."

It is a big deal. She knows her parents make him nervous when Ramona isn't around to act as a buffer. Her mother is always giving him lectures on things like lucid dreaming and Pueblo ceramics, and her father is always trying to get him to study things like tai chi and herbalism. Josh gives her a do-I-have-to? look. "Ah, Mo . . ."

"Please, Josh. It's just Jade today, so you won't be outnumbered. You don't have to get into a long conversation about astral projection. Just tell her you're in a hurry, drop off my stuff, and run."

He can't very well refuse. Not now. Which is what happens when you don't pay attention and get caught. You not only lose those crucial three seconds to come up with a good excuse, you also have to deal with the guilt.

"Okay. Sure." Maybe he can just throw her things from the doorway. *Sorry, Mrs. Minamoto, can't stay . . . emergency in one of the outer galaxies . . .*

But, as things turn out, it is Ramona who has done the throwing; Ramona has inadvertently started the Jenevieve Capistrano ball rolling.

Mrs. Minamoto Adds "Agent of Fate" to Her Many Skills and Talents

Singing a Woody Guthrie song about a hobo to himself, Josh rides into town, the mats slung across his back in their bags and Ramona's canvas satchel holding her yoga gear strapped to the rack over the back wheel. He pulls up in front of the Moon and Sixpence—which the Minamotos call an "arts and crafts gallery" but most everyone else in town calls a store—and locks his bike to a lamppost.

Mrs. Minamoto isn't just a gallery owner (or store-keeper, depending on how you look at it), she's also an artist with an international clientele. One of her "eco-sculptures" is in the front window—a fantastical creature made out of antennae, exhaust pipes, old cans, wires, and plastic hoses—surrounded by more usual crafts such as handmade quilts, small tables carved from tree stumps, hand-blown glasses, and ceramic bowls. There are a few people browsing through the aisles. Jade Minamoto sits in front of the cash register at the jewelry counter on the far side of the room, looking through a magazine. Today, besides her usual armful of silver bangles, several strings of beads, and oversized silver earrings, she wears an intricately patterned scarf (possibly African) around her head, an embroidered blouse (possibly Mexican), and a patchwork Chinese jacket. Ramona's mother is a one-woman global village.

Josh sighs. It's good that there's only one Minamoto in the store, but it would be better if that one Minamoto were busy. Very busy. He likes the Minamotos—you could never accuse them of being unpleasant, and they are definitely interesting—but as much as he likes them, he also finds them intimidating. Or maybe overpowering would be more accurate. If people were birds, most of the citizens of Parsons Falls would be sparrows or robins; the Minamotos would be salmon-crested cockatoos.

The bamboo wind chimes over the entrance sound as he opens the door. Although the Moon and Sixpence specializes in "traditional American crafts," the CD that's playing softly is Tibetan crystal bowl music. You could never accuse them of being narrow in their tastes.

"Josh!" Jade Minamoto jumps from her antique wooden bar stool and charges around the counter to embrace him, nearly lifting him off his feet. Ramona has her father's dark hair and eyes but her mother's large bones. "What a nice surprise! I haven't seen you since our wonderful summer sojourn in the mountains."

Where, besides buying cast-iron parlor stoves and wooden dry sinks, she spent many rainy afternoons communing with the spirits of the forest through meditation.

"No, I guess not." She's the only person who can make him actually chuckle. *Heh-heh-heh* . . . "I've been really busy since we got back."

"Oh, I know, I know . . ." Her bracelets jangle and her earrings swing. "Haven't we all? But the nature of the cosmos is constant change and movement, isn't it? So that's all to the good." Without warning, she grabs his shoulders and holds him at arm's length, scrutinizing him as if the vacation had been three years ago and not three weeks. She has the grip of a sumo wrestler. "How have you been? How's your evolution?" This is what he means. How are you supposed to answer a question like that? *My evolution's progressing nicely, thank you. Any day now I'll be crawling out of the primal swamp?* "And how's the cosmos treating you?"

With its usual indifference. "I'm fine, thanks. I—"

"You know," she says, rushing on as if the buzzer's going to sound and cut her off, "I was thinking about your birth chart. It's one of the most interesting I've come across." Besides being an artist and retailer of exceptional handmade goods, Ramona's mother is an amateur astrologer. There's very little that happens in the world for which Jade Minamoto doesn't hold some poor planet responsible. "I've always felt close to you, Josh, but this really gave me new insights into your character and personality." He's pretty sure that isn't good news. "I'm so glad we finally had the opportunity to sit down and do it."

For which he blames the long mountain nights, the rain, and the lack of TV and computers in the cabin.

"Yeah, me, too." He'd been avoiding it for years. "It was terrific. I never realized how complex astrology is." It certainly put both psychoanalysis and genetics in a new perspective. "But the reason I—"

"You don't fool me." Having released his shoulders, she gives him a playful poke that nearly sends him into a display of baskets. "I know you don't take it any more seriously than Ramona does. She jokes that I'm the Cosmic Cowgirl." Ramona also says she figures it's lucky her mother's not into séances or reading the innards of sacrificial lambs. Those could cause problems. "But astrology is a science almost as old as man himself."

Science! If Einstein hadn't been cremated, he'd be rolling in his grave.

"Speaking of Mo—that's why I'm here." He pulls the purple velvet bag off his shoulder and thrusts it and the canvas satchel at Mrs. Minamoto. "She asked me to bring this by. You know, because she's babysitting and didn't want to carry it around with her."

"Why, that's very kind of you." He's thrusting but she isn't taking. "I hope she didn't put you to any trouble."

"No, no trouble. She's always doing stuff for me." And then, perhaps because that's true, instead of saying that he's in a hurry and can't stay around, he says, "I wasn't doing anything else anyway."

"Well, I'm relieved to hear that." She smiles as shyly as a woman who's as retiring as a hippopotamus can. "In that case, I wonder if I could ask you for another favor, Josh. Just say no if it's too much." As if he could say no to his mother's best friend and live a peaceful, guilt-free life. "You know I'll understand if you can't do it. I don't want to impose. But I was wondering if, perhaps, you could take Ramona's things to the house for me. It would be such a help."

It doesn't strike him as that big a help, since all she has to do is put them in the car when she closes the store and take them out of the car when she gets home, but it seems like such a small thing that he doesn't wonder about it. He thought it was going to be something much, much worse. Go around town collecting garbage for her sculptures. Stay and keep her company in the store for the rest of the day. Name his firstborn Seven Moons.

"Yeah, sure." He slings the mat back over his shoulder. "No sweat."

"And while you're there"—*whop!* it's so fast that he barely hears the trap snap shut behind him—"if you could give Georgia O'Keeffe a little walk? Frank was supposed to be back this morning but he's been held up, and I really can't leave the gallery."

Georgia O'Keeffe in this instance is not the famous modernist painter but the Minamotos' dog. Everything Frank and Jade Minamoto like—from music and art to food and home furnishings—is so esoteric it's astounding they ever found out about it in the first place. Georgia O'Keeffe is no exception. She's small and has a face that looks like someone very heavy sat on it for quite a long time. Georgia often wears ribbons or barrettes to keep her long hair out of her eyes, making her look dainty and demure. People are always cooing over her, *Oh, isn't she adorable*. But she isn't adorable, or dainty and demure. She may be small, but she has the nature of a much larger animal. A lion, say, or a crocodile. She seems to be fond of the Minamotos (at least, she's never bitten one of them), but there is very little else in the world that meets with her approval. She barks at everything—people, moving vehicles, lampposts, balloons, drifting leaves, things that humans can't see—and can't spot another dog without trying to attack it. Especially if it's another dog that's at least twenty times her size. She has never really warmed to Josh either.

"I don't know . . . I mean, I'd love to help you out, Mrs. Minamoto, but Georgia doesn't always listen to me." It once took him twenty minutes just to get her out from under a car. If she was ever sent to obedience school, she was probably expelled.

Georgia O'Keeffe, however, isn't the only one who doesn't listen to Josh. Jade Minamoto has already dashed back to the counter and retrieved the spare house keys. "You just have to assert yourself, Josh. I know you're basically a gentle and unassuming person, but you have to be lead dog. Make her understand you're boss." She shoves the keys into his hand. "Just put on her leash and walk her around the block. She's been cooped up all morning. She'll love you for it."

He looks down at the key ring he's holding. Our Lady of Guadalupe, encased in plastic. Of course. His mother's key ring is from the local garage.

"Don't worry about the keys," says Mrs. Minamoto,

not reading his mind. "You can give them to Ramona at school tomorrow."

She means, if her dog doesn't kill him.

Georgia O'Keeffe—who besides having a disagreeable personality has highly developed senses of smell and of hearing—starts barking before he even steps onto the porch. She is an impressive jumper for an animal with no legs to speak of and hurls herself at his back while he's trying to disarm the alarm. Why bother having an alarm when you have psycho-pooch, who, tired of leaping, attaches herself to his jeans so that he drags her with him as he goes to the kitchen for her leash. What little joy Georgia gets out of life is at least partially about going outside. He picks up the leash, pink like her collar (and all her other accessories, though really they should be black as pitch to match her heart), and as soon as Georgia sees it she lets go of him and throws herself against his legs, yapping hysterically for him to attach it to her collar.

I am lead dog, he tells himself. *I am in control*. He commands her to sit and, miraculously, she does. Probably she's just exhausted herself and is taking a quick break. He fixes her with his sternest look. "I'm warning you," he warns her, "we're going once around the block for you to do your business, and that's all. I don't want any drama. No going after kids on bikes. No running after cars. No harassing Rottweilers. No chasing cats. Nothing. Because if you're going to cause trouble you can stay here."

She seems to accept his terms; she wags her tail.

Their progress from corner to corner is slow but remarkably uneventful. She sniffs and pees, and twice takes a dump, Josh turning his back so he doesn't have to watch, then taking the pink pooper-scooper and slipping the poo into the pink plastic bag with his nose squinched up and his eyes only half open.

The walk goes so well that, even though this wasn't how he planned to spend his afternoon, Josh is humming under his breath an old and very positive song about a dog as they turn back onto the Minamotos' street, and congratulating himself for finally standing up to Georgia O'Keeffe, an animal not much bigger than a cantaloupe. Which is when there is a sudden tug on the leash—and, before he knows what's happened, she's gone in a beige blur. He stands there for several very long seconds, caught in time like a fly in amber, holding air and watching the tawny smudge of fur tear across the road and straight up the oak tree in the middle of the opposite yard, the pink snake of nylon of her leash trailing behind her. Hell and damnation. It's not as if dogs can actually climb trees. She really is the Devil's spawn. Josh races after her, causing a blast of horn and squealing brakes. She's not even on the lowest branch, but two above it, pressed against the trunk of the tree and, for the first time in all the years he's known her, looking worried. Up in the highest branches, a squirrel peers through the leaves, watching. At least she listened when he said not to chase cats.

Josh may not be an athlete, but he has enough agility and strength to pull himself into the tree. He grabs Georgia O'Keeffe, who, along with all her other negative qualities, doesn't like to be held. She squirms, wriggles, and whimpers. She nips at him—shoulder, ear, chin, hand. How the hell is he supposed to get down and hold on to her at the same time unless he simply jumps? He judges the distance between them and the ground. He'll probably break a bone or two, but it's unlikely he'd break his neck. Not impossible, but definitely improbable.

He is trying to decide the best way to throw himself for the minimum injury to both him and the dog when a voice below says, "Hey! You there! You mind if I ask what you're doing in my tree?" It is not what you'd call a friendly voice.

Josh looks down. A man built like a cement wall is glaring up at him. He's wearing heavy green gardening gloves and a heavy black scowl. He's a man who has "lead dog" written all over him.

"What are you, deaf as well as stupid?" Somehow, although the man doesn't raise his voice, he sounds as if he's shouting. "Get down from there this minute! You're trespassing on my property."

This is not a request, it's an order—from a man who is obviously used to giving them and to being obeyed. This, however, is one time when he's going to be disappointed.

"I can't," Josh calls back, as Georgia draws blood from his hand. "I have this dog—"

"Dog?" The man steps closer for a better look at the wriggling mass Josh is clenching. "That's not a dog. It's a toupee with feet."

"Whatever you want to call it, sir, that's fine. But I still can't get down while I'm holding her."

"Don't make me come up after you, young man." This is not a request, either. It's a threat. "Because if you do, it'll be the first time in your life you truly understand what it means to regret something."

Okay, so what does Josh know about trespassing laws? For instance, can he be dragged out of the tree and arrested? He's wondering if this man has the right to injure him if he's unarmed and hasn't actually broken into his home when, like the sun coming out from behind a very large, very dark cloud, a smiling girl steps out from behind the man and says, "It's okay, Dad, I know that boy. He goes to school with me."

Is fear making him hallucinate, or is Jenevieve Capistrano really smiling up at him?

"Hi! It's Josh, right?" He's never looked her straight in the face before. It's a wonder he doesn't fall from his branch like a ripe apple. "What are you doing up there?"

"I'm waiting for a bus," says Josh.

Only Jena laughs.

"He says he can't get down," says her father. Clearly there is room for doubt in his mind if in no one else's. "Because he's holding that ridiculous-looking mutt." If the Capistranos had a dog it would undoubtedly be part wolf.

"You go back to what you were doing," Jenevieve tells her father. "I'll get the ladder and help them down."

Before he lumbers off, her father gives Josh one last glare. "Just make sure you don't break any branches," he says.

Georgia O'Keeffe stops struggling as soon as he hands her to Jena and curls up against her. He isn't sure if dogs can laugh, but if they can this one is definitely laughing at him. He thinks he saw her wink.

Josh comes down the ladder slowly; he's never stood in front of Jenevieve before. She has to look down.

"What a surprise," Jena says when he reaches the ground. "I never expected to find the boy who tried to blow up the science lab in a tree in my front yard."

"It wasn't me," says Josh. "And it was an accident."

He really likes her laugh. If you could bottle it and sell it you could probably bring about world peace. At least for a day or two.

"And this is the dog from across the street." She hugs Georgia and kisses the top of her head. Georgia's tail waves like happiness. "She's adorable."

No, she isn't, but she's definitely lucky, being hugged and kissed by Jenevieve Capistrano. Who would ever have thought he could envy that smushed-face creature?

"Yeah. The Minamotos. I was walking her for them. But she got away."

"The Minamotos. Of course. They own that cool store in town." Her smile hovers over Georgia O'Keeffe's head. He never noticed the dimples before. "So you must be friends with the daughter? I don't really know her, but I've seen her around. And we're both in the drama club. The really tall girl with those amazing eyebrows and that great mouth?"

"Ramona." If asked, Josh would have said that

Ramona definitely has eyebrows and a mouth, but he never really noticed how amazing or great they are. Then for some reason, he feels the need to add, "And I'm friends with her parents, too. Our moms are really close."

She nods, sunlight sparkling off the pink in her hair. They stand there smiling at each other for a few seconds. He can't seem to find anything else to say, but he doesn't want to go.

And then Jena comes to his rescue for the second time. "Hey, you want a drink?" she asks. "You must be thirsty after climbing up that tree."

He would drink ditchwater if she were offering. "Oh, I don't—I wouldn't want to put you to any trouble."

"It's no trouble."

His eyes dart around the lawn. He's not so sure her father would want him in his house any more than he wanted him in his tree.

"Don't worry about Dad. His bark is worse than his bite."

Which is not something you could say about Georgia O'Keeffe.

The Ball Continues to Roll

Josh and Carver are leaving school together — Carver to go to the dentist and Josh into town to pick up the new harmonica he ordered. Carver is talking about a recent article he read on fracking when he suddenly breaks off, comes to a stop, claps Josh on the shoulder and says, "Am I losing my mind, or did I just see you wave to Tilda Kopel?" He couldn't look more shocked if he'd seen Josh shaking hands with the CEO of Shell Oil. "What happened? You sell her your soul?"

"No, of course not. The invisibility shield finally wore off and she can see me now." Carver doesn't laugh. "Oh, for Christ's sake, I wasn't waving to Tilda."

"Well, it sure looked like you were waving to her. I thought the apocalypse was upon us."

"Well, I wasn't." Jenevieve was just about to get into the Kopel BMW. "I was waving to the girl with her."

Carver looks over at the car, but it is already going down the drive and there is nothing to see but the backs of heads. He turns to Josh. "Who?"

"That new girl. Jena Capistrano."

"You mean the one with the My Little Pony hair thing going on?"

That's what comes of having sisters; Josh just thought it was pink. He nods. "That's her."

"I didn't know you knew her." Carver doesn't look shocked now, he looks curious. Possibly suspicious.

"I don't *know* her. She's in my language arts class."

"And?"

Possibly very suspicious.

"And nothing. I ran into her the other day when I was walking the Minamotos' dog. Well, actually, it wasn't like I ran into her, it was more like Georgia O'Keeffe ran up a tree on the Capistranos' lawn and I had to go after her." He explains about Jena's father and the ladder and her offering him a drink. "So that's how I got to know her. Kind of."

Getting to know her being the operative words. Josh is even less a fan of Rodgers and Hammerstein than he is of the Beatles, but there seems to be something about Jenevieve Capistrano that reminds him of songs he barely knows and never liked. The show tune "Getting to Know You," of which he can sing exactly twenty-one words (though he has no idea how he knows that many of them), is the song that played in his head all the way home on the afternoon he climbed down the Capistranos' ladder to spend half an hour in the Capistranos' kitchen.

"You sure know how to impress a girl," says Carver. "What are you planning to do next? Go down her chimney?"

It's an idea. If he weren't afraid of finding Jena's father waiting for him with a loaded gun he might actually consider it. Because the pathetic truth is that he doesn't know what to do next. The half hour or so that he spent with her was easy. They talked effortlessly; he made her laugh. The fact that she obviously enjoyed his company made him fearless—and, even if he's the only witness to it, pretty entertaining and charming as well. But it was like something out of a fantasy. One in which the young, hapless hero climbs a tree and finds himself in a magical kingdom where things he's only dreamed about exist. Now, however, he is in the real world again—and doesn't know how to get back.

But, if nothing else, Josh now knows a lot more about Jenevieve Capistrano than he did before. He knows that her father was an army officer and that she's lived in half a dozen states and three other countries. "It's not nearly as interesting as you think," said Jena. "It just means I know a little bit about a lot of places, but no place really well." This time it's going to be different. Her father—the General, as she calls him, because people called him that so much when she was little that she thought it was his name—took early retirement and a desk job. "It's just too bad it was my mom dying made him do that," said Jena. "She would've liked Parsons Falls."

Josh's father had a heart attack in his car; Jena's mother was hit by a truck. Which makes them both half orphans. Jena said she hoped they had more in common than that. "You mean besides the possibility of both of us being related to Genghis Khan?" joked Josh. Jena said, "Genghis who?"

But it turned out she was right: they did have more in common than the death of a parent in an automobile and a thirteenth-century Mongolian warrior. Not a lot more, maybe, but more than the casual observer might suppose. She's never heard of Robert Johnson, but she does like *Star Trek* and loves old movies. She discovered them both when she was in a new place and had nothing to do but watch TV. And her favorite soft drink is cream soda—which Josh is sure would be his if he drank soda.

They got on well. Like friends—or people who could be friends. But where does he go from here? And how does he get there? He wishes someone would write a book, *Dating for Absolute Dummies*. Advice on what to say, what not to say, and what to do if you don't have the nerve to ask someone out but think you might like to. Probably someone has written it. Not that that helps him. He can't buy it online for fear that his mother would find out. She uses his computer; she'd be bound to notice the barrage of ads for similar products that follows any purchase. She'd want to know what he's up to—she may look like a regular mother, but she has the mind of a secret agent. The bookstore at the mall is also out. He only shops at the mall if the alternative is death by stampeding cattle, but even if he *were* desperate enough, it's too risky. With his luck he'd be waiting to pay when Tilda Kopel walked in and saw him; it'd be all over the school before he finished counting his change. And he can't very well go to the library and take it out under the gimlet gaze of Mrs. Batista, either. She knew him when he was reading Dr. Seuss. She also knows his mother well enough to say something to her. Which would make his mother think that it's time for another talk about sex, birth control, and sexually transmitted diseases. He isn't sure he could survive another one. No, Josh is on his own, a solitary explorer in a dark, uncharted land. A dark, uncharted land that is heavily guarded and patrolled.

He would happily have spent the whole afternoon in

the Capistranos' kitchen getting to know Jena, but her father had other ideas. There was still half a glass of apple juice in front of Josh when the General marched in. He'd ditched the gardening gloves, but he still wore the scowl. Apparently Josh hadn't made a very good first impression.

"Dad!" At least one of them was glad to see him. "You haven't been introduced. This is Josh Shine." She turned the spotlight of her smile on Josh. "This is my dad—"

"General Capistrano," said her father.

Should he salute? Probably not. Stand up? To do what, sit down again? He was too far away for a handshake. A headshake would have to do. "Pleased to meet you, sir."

The second impression was no improvement on the first. The General also nodded, but didn't suggest by word or expression that he was pleased to meet Josh.

"I'm sorry about climbing your tree, but the dog . . ."

The General, however, was no longer looking at Josh, which had the effect of making him disappear. "Came in for my lunch," he said to Jena, and looked from her to the clock on the wall.

This statement was followed by a silence so awkward it was virtually tripping on its own feet and knocking over everything not nailed down.

"Gosh, is that the time?" Josh stood up. "I better get going."

The last thing Jena said when she showed him out was, "It was really nice talking to you."

And she hasn't talked to him since. She waves. She smiles. When he or someone else says something funny in class, she looks his way. But except for a quick nod or low "Hi!" if they pass in the hall, not a word has been exchanged. How could it be? She's always with Tilda Kopel: part bodyguard, part white noise. He can tell from the way Tilda glares over his head (the closest she's ever come to meeting his eyes) that she doesn't approve of even that little communication between Jena and him. If he could get Jena alone for just ten minutes, then maybe they could pick up where they left off. He's been praying all week that Tilda would catch the flu that's been going around, but her immune system seems to be as strong as her ego.

Josh comes out of the music store, slipping the harmonica box into his satchel. He can't wait to get home to try it out, and starts to stride up the street when, suddenly, there's Jena, coming out of the deli. She sees him at the same second that he sees her, but though he stops short, unsure what to do next, she hurries toward him. "Josh! Hi!"

He says, "Hi!" And then, because he's been caught off guard and can't think of anything else, says, "Your hair doesn't have any pink in it anymore." Just in case she hasn't noticed.

"I washed it out." She holds up one hand. "Now the only pink on me is my nails." The same shade as Tilda Kopel's, though this is not something Josh would be likely to notice. "The hair was just a spray. It was the thing to do at my last school but Tilda says it's way passé."

He liked it, but what does he know? His mother still trims his hair.

Jena says she's really glad she ran into him. She enjoyed talking to him the other day.

"Me, too." Out of the corner of his eye, he looks for Tilda Kopel. She has to be around here somewhere, ready to pounce. "I never get a chance to talk to you at school. We're always rushing off to class or whatever." The whatever being Tilda, of course.

Jena shrugs. "I guess that's why they call it school. Because of all the classes."

"And here I thought it was because of all the fish," says Josh.

There's a second's time lapse between the joke and her laughter. "You have such a different sense of humor than most people I know."

"That's what they said about King Henry the Eighth," says Josh, and she laughs again.

She thinks he's really funny. "Nobody's ever made me laugh so much. Except on TV or in a movie." And then, while he's convincing himself that she means this in a good way—that she's laughing with him, not at him—she suggests that they go to Hava Java for a coffee. "We deserve it. End of the week chill-out."

Which must mean that Tilda Kopel isn't going to suddenly pop out from under a manhole cover, or Jena would be chilling out with her.

He doesn't fight the temptation to look behind him as if she must be talking to someone else. "Hava Java?" He makes a thinking-about-it face.

"Besides, the General's working late tonight." Jena makes an I-know-I'm-being-silly-but face. "I don't want you to think I'm a baby or anything, but I don't like to be in the house by myself for hours and hours. It kind of creeps me out." She gives him a smile that practically melts his bones. "I'd rather hang out with you."

I'd rather hang out with you. . . . This isn't something he ever expected to hear from Jenevieve Capistrano (or anyone like her) but he's not about to argue. Never mind trying out his new harmonica. He wouldn't say no to her if the ghost of the renowned blues harp player Paul Butterfield were waiting at home to give him a lesson.

"Sure." Amazingly enough, he still has the power of

speech. "Sounds good to me. I'm always up for chilling out at the end of the week." *As if.*

Hava Java is where the popular kids go; needless to say, he's never been there before.

Jena picks a table by the window. "I really am glad I ran into you," she says as soon as they sit down. She takes up a packet of sugar. "I've been wanting to apologize."

Whatever it is she's responsible for—global warming, species extinction, another futile war—he forgives her.

"For what?"

She puts the sugar back and looks at Josh. "For my dad. The way he acted the other day. He can be a little heavy-handed sometimes. He's not really used to being a single parent." She picks up a different sugar packet this time. "Since my mom died he's kind of overprotective. You know, 'cause I'm all he's got."

Overprotective as in, if he wanted to kill an ant, he'd use a tank. Josh is all his mother has, but she tries to ignore him as much as she can.

"It's okay, Jena." Josh laughs. "If I were your dad, I wouldn't like me, either."

It was supposed to be a joke, but Jena winces. "It's not that he really dislikes you . . ."

Which is the same as saying he doesn't really like Josh. Just wait till he gets to know him.

"Because I was in his tree? Is he holding that against me? It wasn't really my fault—and I did say I was sorry. It's not like I'm a tree-hugger or anything like that." Can the General possibly know that his best friend is Carver, dedicated hugger of trees?

"Oh, I know you're not. And I'm sure he knows it was just . . . you know . . . one of those weird things that happen . . ." Though, obviously, not to General Capistrano. "But it's not just the tree." Her eyes are on his hands. "You know . . . my dad's kind of straight army." And expects everyone else to be straight army, too; especially if they're friends of hers. "And, you know . . . you have a ponytail."

It's a very small ponytail. More a My Little Pony tail. You'd think he'd be okay with that. "You had pink hair."

"That was just a fad. He could live with a few streaks now and then."

"Right. So that's why he doesn't like me? Because I tie my hair back? Is that a crime somewhere?" Thank God he hasn't seen Josh when he holds it back with a headband.

"No, of course not. It's just, you know, odd. Kind of hippie."

"Hippie? The Founding Fathers wore their hair tied back." Though not with headbands. "They weren't hippies. You've never seen a picture of Jefferson in a tie-dyed T-shirt."

She doesn't laugh; maybe he's stopped being funny. "Well, no . . ." She's on her third sugar packet. "But also . . . you know . . . he noticed the yoga mat."

"The yoga mat?" A right the Founding Fathers with their ponytails forgot to put in the Constitution. "What made him so sure it wasn't a rifle?" You can bear arms but not yoga mats.

This time he does make her laugh again. "Because if it was a rifle my dad would've shot you out of that tree."

Here's a valuable piece of information that could come in very handy in future encounters with the General. Don't do anything to provoke him.

"So what's wrong with the yoga mat?"

"Nothing. Not really. I think it's cool you do yoga. Totally. You're the only guy I've ever known who does it." Obviously, she's never met Sting, rock legend and yogini. "Only, you know . . . my dad doesn't think it's very masculine. Not like qigong or kung fu. He can tell you're not military material."

A man as perceptive as he is opinionated and large.

"You mean you're only allowed to talk to trained killers? Isn't that a little limiting?"

She tugs on her hair. "Oh, you know what I mean. The General thinks boys should be clean-cut and play football and stuff like that. You're a little—"

"Short?" guesses Josh. "Bent-nosed? Pointy-eared? Near-sighted?"

"Oh God . . ." Suddenly her laugh sounds like an itch. "I wasn't being critical. I wish I'd never said anything."

She isn't the only one. If they keep this up the General isn't going to be alone in thinking that Josh is substandard. Before he completely loses every drop of confidence he has, Josh volunteers to get their drinks. She wants a cappuccino and a banana-split brownie with two forks—they're so good he just has to try it. He decides not to mention his lack of enthusiasm for both bananas and chocolate.

She stares at the tray as he sets it on the table. Curiously. As if she was expecting something else. "What's that in your cup?"

"Tea. It's the ancient drink of the Chinese, believed to have medicinal properties."

"Wow." He can't tell if she's impressed or simply astonished. "I didn't even know they had tea here." She peers into his cup as if it might be filled with grubs. She sniffs. "What kind of tea is that? It smells funny."

"It's green tea." He hands Jena her cappuccino. "With jasmine."

"Green tea? Really?" She couldn't sound more astounded if he'd told her it was yak milk. "You don't drink coffee?"

"It's against my religion."

"Really?"

"No. I just don't like it."

"See, that's another thing the General would think is weird."

Tea, yoga, and enough hair to wrap an elastic band around. It's amazing Josh's mother lets him go out by himself.

"That I don't drink coffee?" The General's spectrum for normal behavior is clearly a small one. "Is that what he thinks I am? Weird?"

She answers the question he didn't ask. "But I don't. I don't know anybody like you."

He thinks she means this in a good way. Hopes; hopes she means it in a good way. "That's not the same as weird?"

"Of course not! It just means you're different. You know, from the people I'm used to." If her smile were an ocean he would definitely drown. He would probably drown if it were a puddle. "My dad has all these rules. Rules for every occasion. It's like everything has to fit in a box. And I get it. I understand why."

He doesn't say, *Really? You do? Could you explain it to me?* He nods as if he gets it, too.

"But I think you're kind of cool."

"Only kind of?"

"Cool and funky."

Funky is absolutely good. Bluesmen are supposed to be funky. And cool. Eat your heart out, General Capistrano. Go put that in a box.

He sits across from her, sipping his tea and wielding his fork, not worrying about what chocolate does to his skin or whether or not the eggs were free-range or came from chickens who lived short, miserable lives in tiny cages—which he would be if Carver were here. So this must be what it's like to be an average teenager, hanging out in the trendy coffee shop, eating brownies sweet enough to make your teeth scream. Another song he doesn't like and didn't know he knew pops into his head: "If My Friends Could See Me Now." Though not Carver; Carver would be in the kitchen, checking out the eggs.

Jena does most of the talking.

Josh is used to talking to the guys. Movies. Games. School. Funny stories. Music. TV shows. Bulletins on hunger. Families and extraterrestrials. How many species go extinct every day, how much plastic is in the oceans and the ethics of artificial intelligence (Carver); the difficulties of intergalactic colonization, conspiracy theories, art house vs. Hollywood movies and whether or not Martin Scorsese has peaked (Sal). None of them are really into cars or motorcycles, but they make up for that with conversations on bicycle maintenance and space travel. Indeed, if you don't count Josh's mother, Ramona is the only other female he's ever conversed with regularly and at length—and Jena, of course, is nothing like Ramona. Ramona's interests are eclectic, to say the least—ranging from the history of clothes and the development of music to *barro negro* pottery and *The Simpsons*. When they were up at the Minamotos' cabin last summer, he and Ramona had a two-hour discussion one evening about anchorites. It was interesting at the time—she knew a lot more about them than he would have thought—but it wasn't what most people would expect from a teenage girl. Jena, however, talks about regular, everyday things—movies and TV shows he's never watched, bands and singers he's never heard of, books he'll never read—never once mentioning an obscure composer or the Coen brothers or the latest scientific report on the effects of habitat destruction. She does, like Ramona, mention the school play—but, unlike Ramona, she loves *Bye Bye Birdie*. Jena has to be the most normal person he knows. Which is something else he likes about her. Normal people don't usually gravitate toward him. He doesn't wonder why she does.

"You know, I'm really glad you climbed our tree," says

Jena over their second drink. "Or we might never have become friends."

Friends. They've become friends. It wasn't so hard after all.

"Me, too." He'll never say another bad thing about the Minamotos or their dog—not even if Georgia O'Keeffe bites him again.

"You're easy to talk to. You know, for a boy."

Josh laughs. "Right." Like Jenevieve Capistrano has had no practice talking to boys. "Is that because I look more like an owl?"

"No, you idiot." She flicks a brownie crumb at him. "It's just—I don't know, boys . . ." She shrugs. "It's nice to just be friends with a guy, without wondering what his motives are. 'Cause there's always something. You think you're just watching a movie together and the next thing he's sticking his tongue in your mouth." From her expression you'd think her coffee was sour. "Or you send them a picture or tell them a secret and the next thing you know it's all over the Internet. I mean, that never happened to me, but it's happened to girls I know. It can be really creepy and gross. So it makes you cautious, you know? Only, I can tell you're not like that."

He couldn't be, not even if he was really as devious as the Snake in the Garden. He doesn't do social media.

"Not at all? Are you serious?"

"Absolutely." And he paraphrases Emily Dickinson's poem about not wanting to be public like a frog and admired by the bog. "Ribbit."

Her smile feels as if she's squeezed his hand. "Wow. You are really different. Maybe that's why talking to you is like talking to a girlfriend."

Is that a compliment? It has to be a compliment. Maybe. He thinks of the popular boys at school, but can't imagine anyone telling any of them that talking to him is like talking to a girl. Not without getting hit.

"You do know I'm not a cross-dresser, right?" Leaning forward with a mock-serious face. "There'll be no borrowing my clothes or anything like that."

Jena grins. "You see what I mean?"

No. He might as well be blindfolded with a bag over his head. "I'm not sure. Not a hundred percent."

"Well . . ." There is a thin moustache of foam over her upper lip. If it were on him he'd look like a clown; it just makes her look cuter. "I guess what I mean is because I know you're not going to hit on me, I can just chill. You know, be myself."

This is good. It has to be good. He doesn't make her feel like a hunted animal. He doesn't even have to ask himself how she knows this about him. It must be obvious. Which means that, on the other side of the coin, this isn't good. He doesn't stand the chance of an ice cube in a pizza oven with a girl like her. If he ever does get a girlfriend, it will have to be someone who can't get anyone else either.

"Me, too." He winks. "I know you won't believe this, seeing as I'm so handsome, charming, and sophisticated, but talking to girls isn't really my area of expertise."

"Oh, I don't know. You seem to be doing okay to me." She takes another sip of her coffee. "What about Ramona? I see you talking to her."

"Minamoto?" As if the school is crammed to the roof with girls named Ramona. "Ramona and I are just friends."

Her smile is a wink. "You mean, she's like your guy buddies?"

"Except that she's taller, wears dresses, and is more discreet about farting, yeah."

"She sure doesn't look like a guy," says Jena.

Girls Are Full of Surprises

She calls him the next morning. His mother is at the kitchen table, rewiring an old lamp she bought in the summer, so Josh and Charley Patton are sitting side by side at the breakfast bar, sharing a slice of toast. When the landline rings, he is wiping blueberry jam from Charley Patton's nose and doesn't even look up since it can't be for him. His friends only call him on his cell.

His mother answers, thinking it's for her. "Hello." Her eyes dart to Josh. "Just a minute. He's right here. I'll get him." She puts her hand over the mouthpiece. "It's for you." She already has that mother's what's-going-on? look on her face. "It's a girl." Said with the same restrained surprise as if she'd announced *It's the President*.

So it isn't Mo. Not counting girls who ask him questions about the math homework (who would never think of calling him) and Aya and Hazel from the chess club (who would also call him on his cell phone), Josh only knows one other girl who might possibly want to speak to him. But of course it can't be her. There's no way on this planet it could be her. It must be someone who wants to join the chess club and was given this number by the advisor. Nevertheless, he gets up so fast he nearly knocks Charley Patton off his stool.

"Hi!" says Jena. "It's me. I hope you don't mind. I got your number from Ramona."

Of course she did. Why look it up when you can just walk across the street and ask Ramona?

"Oh, hi. No, that's okay." He turns his back on his mother. "What's up?"

"Nothing really. I was just wondering if you're doing anything tonight."

As unlikely as it seems, she has to be talking to him. "Me?"

"It's just that I have this DVD of some really old Hitchcocks. And you know, I was thinking maybe you'd want to watch them with me."

Do birds sing?

"You said you like old movies, right?"

"I did say that. I do."

"If you aren't busy. But probably you already have plans. It's pretty last-minute. Saturday night."

Should he play it cool?

"Well . . . I don't know. . . . I'll have to consult my calendar. . . . Hmmm . . . Looks like you're in luck, I think I can squeeze you in."

"That's great," says Jena. "I'll see you around seven? You remember where I live, right?"

"Sure," says Josh. "The house with the tree."

As soon as he hangs up, his mother says, "So who was that?"

There are many advantages to being an only child—privacy, no one with whom you have to share everything, no one who borrows your things all the time or bosses you around, no rivalry for affection—but there are times when Josh wouldn't mind having a few siblings to distract his mother's attention from him. And this, of course, is one of those times. If he had nine brothers and sisters, the President could call him and she wouldn't notice.

He turns around. She's smiling as though she asked an innocent question, but the screwdriver's pointing at him like a finger.

"Nobody. Just a girl. From school."

"And does this girl have a name?"

No.

"Yeah, sure she does. It's Jena."

"Jena Capistrano?" How does she know that? How

can she know that? Josh stares at his mother as if she has just revealed herself as the ancient goddess Isis. Disguised as a mild-mannered school librarian . . . "The girl who just moved into the Featherlanes' old house? Across from the Minamotos?"

He could have saved a lot of time by asking his mother to introduce him to Jena.

"Yeah. That's her."

"She's cute." Hannah smiles as if she's trying not to laugh out loud. Smirking. That's what she's doing; his mother's smirking at him.

"It's nothing like that," says Josh. "We're just friends."

"Jade says the father seems a little rigid and authoritarian."

"He was in the army."

"And the army's still in him, according to Jade." She puts down the screwdriver, ready to chat. "So what's the daughter like? It can't be easy for her, losing her mother like that. And I bet he's not easy either—or used to being the go-to parent." Is there anything this woman doesn't know?

This time it's his phone that rings. Thank God. He grabs it from the counter as if he's snatching it from the path of an oncoming train, and turns his back on his mother again.

"So what's with you and bird girl?" Ramona, of course, would know all about the swallows returning to Capistrano—her musical knowledge is also eclectic. Nor is she a girl to chase you around the bush if she can simply trample the bush into the ground and confront you directly. "You know she came over and asked me for your number."

"Yeah, she said." Of the scores of things it never occurs to Josh to wonder about right now is why Ramona gave Jena the number for the landline and not the one for his cell. "Nothing's with us. We're just friends. She's in Burleigh's class with me. She wanted to know something about the homework."

"Really?" He has the feeling Ramona may be smirking, too. "I saw you guys in HJ yesterday."

Of course she did. This is what he means about life being ironic. It just never lets up.

"Did you?"

"Uh-huh. You were right in the window. Like you were dummies advertising back-to-school clothes. Well, not you. But she could've been."

One of the problems with living in a small town is, of course, that it's small. And, in this case, laid out in such a way that anyone looking out the window of the Moon and Sixpence would have a good view of anyone sitting in the window of the coffee shop across the street.

"Were we robbing the place or were we just drinking coffee?" asks Josh.

"I don't know about her," says Ramona, "but you don't drink coffee. So probably you were having tea. But I guess you were too busy talking for her to ask you about the homework then." Definitely. Mo is definitely smirking. "Or your phone number."

"Yeah," says Josh. "I guess we were."

Ramona sits at the counter of the Moon and Sixpence, working on a display of macramé jewelry. Her mother has gone to choose some handmade wooden bowls, and the sales assistant called in sick, so Ramona has been left in charge. It's a quiet afternoon, which suits Ramona's mood. Museful. She can't stop thinking about Jenevieve Capistrano and Josh. Ramona is used to thinking about Josh, but until yesterday the only thoughts she had about the new girl were that she should do all her hair pink (it makes her look way more interesting) and that it's too bad she's already tight with Tilda Kopel, because, like being born a princess, it ruins your chances for a normal life. Which isn't what Ramona's thinking now. *Why were Josh and Jena in Hava Java together yesterday? Why did Jena want his phone number? What's going on?* Ramona tells herself that nothing's going on. They're in the same language arts class. They happened to be in town at the same time yesterday. They ran into each other. They decided to go for a drink. For God's sake, what's the big deal? This is the twenty-first century. A girl and boy can go to a café together without a chaperone. It doesn't mean anything. It's normal. Everybody does stuff like that all the time. She starts fastening bracelets on a papier-mâché arm, lining them up one on top of another like a rainbow.

But Josh doesn't do stuff like that. Maybe with girls from the chess club, but not with someone in Tilda Kopel's group. Especially someone who, if you ask Ramona, is starting to resemble Tilda more and more with every passing day. She holds up two bracelets, deciding which to put on next—the all-white strings with quartz and silver beads or the blues and greens with turquoise and gold? And anyway, what does she care? If Josh wants to hang out with someone who probably can't tell a guitar from a mandolin, that's his business. Not Ramona's. She chooses the bracelet of blues and greens and fastens it around the arm. Besides, he could never be *interested* interested in a Kopel clone. *Seriously?* Just the thought makes her laugh. She is so not his type. And there's sure as hell no way Jenevieve Capistrano would be interested in him. Tilda doesn't speak to Josh. She's made fun of and laughed at him quite a few times over the years, but she's never exchanged words. And even if Jena did like him, she couldn't have the social life she has with Josh around. If they went to games he'd fall asleep. And what about parties and dances? Josh's idea of dressed-up is clean jeans and his father's red suspenders; he doesn't even own a suit. She's smiling to herself at the idea of Josh at the prom when the bamboo wind chimes knock together gently as the door opens. Ramona looks over, still smiling.

Sal smiles back. He saw her through the window and thought he'd stop by and say hi. "Hi," says Sal. And then, having temporarily run out of words, waves.

Just dropping by like this isn't something Sal has ever done before, not unless he was with Josh, but things have changed, of course—now that Ramona and Sal are both involved in the musical, they have another connection. Ramona waves back. "Hi." She likes Sal and is glad to see him, though the truth is that she'd be glad to see a moose walk through the door right now—anything to distract her from thinking about Jenevieve and Josh.

Sal comes up beside her, jamming his hands in his pockets. He asks where her mother is. He admires the jewelry. He admires the display. He talks about the changes Mr. Boxhill's making in the play. All the while he shifts from foot to foot, as if he's balancing on a raft. And then he says, sounding surprised at himself, "Hey, I just had an idea. If you're not busy tonight I have a couple of sixties movies I got for research. You could come over and see them with me. They might give you some ideas. You know, for costumes."

"That's a great idea. I'd love to." Before those words make him too happy, she adds, "But I can't. Zara's coming over tonight."

"Zara." He thinks this over for a second, then smiles. "Zara. Right. I guess I should've known."

"Maybe another time," says Ramona.

"Yeah, okay. That'd be chill. Another time." He rocks on his heels and doesn't ask her when.

Now arranging earrings on a velvet-covered board, Ramona wants to know what happened to boys' night in. "I thought you guys always get together on Saturday nights."

"We do," says Sal. "But Josh had to bail. And Carver got landed with babysitting his sisters. I mean, I could go over there, but we won't be able to watch anything with them around. And we can't lock ourselves in his room—they need supervision."

"What's wrong with Josh?" Very carefully and precisely, she pins a pair of dangling silver-and-turquoise earrings on the board. "How come he bailed?"

"Not sure." She isn't looking at him, but Sal shrugs anyway. "All he said was something came up. I don't know if it's the band or the chess gang."

"It must be pretty important," says Ramona. "It's not like Josh to be so last-minute." His lists of things to do are always in order of importance or urgency. His middle name isn't Spontaneity; it's David.

"Who knows?" says Sal. "Shit happens."

Later, waiting for Zara, Ramona thinks she hears a car pull up outside and looks out her bedroom window. This would be another example of what Josh means when he talks about the ironies of life. Ramona is just in time to see Josh himself turn into the Capistranos' driveway and walk up the path to the front door. No chessboard or guitar in sight.

Shit sure does happen.

As she turns away, Ramona wonders what Tilda Kopel will say about this. Which is a thought that makes her smile.

One Thing Leads to Another, as Things Do

Josh is late. He's almost never late — not unless someone else is involved — and he absolutely didn't want to be late tonight. He wanted to arrive at seven o'clock exactly, to show her he's dependable, the boy you can count on not to let you down. But it took him so long to get ready (choosing his clothes, checking teeth and hair and ears, wishing he looked like someone else) that it's seven thirty before he reaches the Capistranos' front door. Once there, he gazes zombie-like at the house number for several seconds, suddenly unaccountably nervous. What if he farts? What if he smells? *For Pete's sake, it's not a date*, he tells himself. *You're just watching a movie. Think of her as one of the guys. Pretend she's Mo.*

As soon as he rings the bell he hears Jena shout, "I'll get it, Dad! It's for me!" Which is when he remembers the General, Parsons Falls' answer to Darth Vader — and a very good reason for feeling nervous. What if the General shoots him? He automatically takes a step backward, and loses his footing. He's picking himself up from the flower bed when Jena opens the door with a glad-to-see-you smile on her face that immediately turns to a look of concern. "What happened? Are you okay?"

She's not Mo. Mo would have laughed and thanked him for dropping by.

"Yeah, I'm fine. I just missed the step."

The smile returns. "Well, come on in. You're right on time."

She moves back to let him pass her. She lowers her voice and leans towards him so he can feel her breath on his cheek. "Don't worry, my dad'll be leaving in a few minutes." Saturday is the General's poker night. Normally she'd do something with Tilda, but Tilda has a hot date. He should have known. "So I'm really glad you could come so last-minute." Jena makes a face. "I really hate being by myself all night."

She really must, he thinks. *To ask me over.* But immediately banishes that thought as unworthy of her.

"Then it's lucky that you don't have to be," says Josh.

"But besides that, I've really been looking forward to seeing these. My dad only likes guy movies, and Tilda thinks old is anything made more than three years ago.

I know I could watch them by myself, but that's not as much fun."

"You need a cat." Josh follows her down the hallway. "Charley Patton'll watch anything. Especially if there are chips and salsa involved."

"Charley Patton?" Her smile is uncertain. "That's your cat's name?" When she was little she had had a cat called Fluffy because it was. He explains that Charley Patton's named after one of his musical heroes. "Because he really plays a mean guitar."

She's laughing as they enter the kitchen, where the General is putting a six-pack of beer into a cooler bag.

"You remember Josh," says Jena. So brightly you'd think that might be a good thing.

Her father nods at Josh, making it clear that he remembers him vividly and that he's being polite because he loves his daughter, his smile slight enough to be considered no more than a suggestion.

If Josh were any more nervous, he'd probably pass out. He doesn't want to do anything to give the General a reason to ban him from the house, so tries some politeness of his own. "It's nice to see you again, General Capistrano," he lies. And has to stop himself from adding a line he must have heard in some hokey old movie: *Don't worry, sir, I'll take good care of your daughter.*

The way Jena's father is eyeing him, Josh expects him to ask if he's climbed any more trees lately, or why he doesn't cut his hair or take up kickboxing. Instead he asks him what he thinks about the Packers' chances in this year's Super Bowl. Josh doesn't really hear the question, just *Super Bowl*. Football—he's asking him something about football. He might as well ask him who won the Miss America title in 1974. Which isn't to say that Josh isn't aware of the Super Bowl—there isn't a blade of grass in the country that hasn't heard of the Super Bowl—but he has never watched it or any other football game—and is so thrown by the question that he can't think of any reply. He just stands there, looking like an ad for teeth whitening.

Jena rushes into the silence. "Josh is captain of the chess team," she says. "He's not really into sports."

The General puts on his baseball cap. "Somehow that doesn't surprise me."

He has to say something—something to correct the impression that he knows nothing about the sweaty, bloody world of real men. "You know," says Josh, "Napoléon played chess."

Both Capistranos look at him blankly, as if the words came out in the wrong language.

"Bonaparte," clarifies Josh. "Napoléon Bonaparte played chess. The French general?"

"Did he?" General Capistrano picks up his cooler bag and gives Jena a kiss on the cheek. "I better get going." Does he raise his voice slightly? He glances at Josh, the grinning fool with the ponytail. "Don't want to be late," he says. Is there a warning in his tone? *Make sure you behave yourself—or else.*

Neither of them speaks as the General marches from the house, the back door slamming behind him, their eyes fixed on the spot where he was only seconds ago, as if he might suddenly return. Not until they hear the engine start up do they look at each other.

And now they're alone. Really alone for the first time. Alone without a room full of people around them or her father lurking outside. No Tilda Kopel giving him the stink eye when he speaks to Jena or acting as if his voice is the same as silence. The emptiness of the house surrounds them. Jena is definitely not one of the guys—for one thing, none of them wears slippers that look like turquoise Tribbles—and there's no way Josh can pretend that she is. He doesn't know what to do with himself. If he had his guitar with him he'd probably start playing.

She's the first to break the silence. "Hey," says Jena. "Let's get the snacks and start the show."

He watches her open a cabinet and take two bags from a shelf he couldn't reach unless he was standing on something. Then he starts looking around, noticing things he didn't see the first time he was here; he was too busy looking at her. Jena opens another cabinet, takes out two bowls, and turns to find him staring at a photo held to the door of the fridge in a magnetic frame. It's a picture of her and her parents, standing in front of palm trees. The sun is shining and they are all smiling like nothing bad could ever happen to them.

"That was taken a couple of weeks before the accident," says Jena, in a faraway voice he hasn't heard before.

He looks at her, but doesn't know what to say that wouldn't sound as if he was reading it off a greeting card. There is a similar photograph on the mantelpiece in the Shines' living room. Josh, his mother, his father, and Charley Patton sitting on the sofa the day they brought Charley Patton home from the animal shelter. Josh's father isn't in the photograph of Charley Patton's birthday celebration a year later.

"You know, it's funny . . ." Jena's eyes are on the snapshot in its plastic heart-shaped frame, "but even though it's different now"—she puts the bowls on the counter so softly they might be made of foam—"you know, the missing her and everything—it doesn't really get better. It's like I have a hole in my heart."

This he does know.

Josh nods. "Some days I still can't believe my dad is dead." On worse days he can.

She turns away and starts opening the bags, concentrating on getting the chips and pretzels into the bowls without any of them escaping.

He has to change the subject; if they keep on like this they'll both be so depressed he'll wind up going home.

"I notice your dad goes for the minimalist approach to interior decoration," says Josh. There is nothing on the walls of the hall, and the living room looks to be mainly furniture. "My mom's the opposite. She even has things on the ceilings."

Jena laughs. "We're still not totally unpacked. We have boxes of stuff in the cellar and the attic, but we haven't had a chance to get at them somehow. There's always other stuff to do."

"You haven't really been here that long. Plus your dad must be pretty busy with his new job and everything."

"Totally. He's, like, super not used to the civilian world. He's having some adjustment issues."

Josh bets he is. The General probably can't figure out why no one salutes him anymore. The civilian world is probably having some adjustment issues of its own.

"And you have plenty to do just settling into school. I'd hate to have to move like you just did. I'm really impressed by how quickly you've made friends." She has a lot more friends than he has. "It can't be easy, starting all over in a new town where you don't know anybody or anything." He makes the face of the boy who sat by himself, walked by himself, and ate by himself on the third-grade trip to the natural history museum because Carver was out with the measles. "God knows I've always found school life hard enough, and I've known most of these people for years and years."

He would probably go to school dressed as a chicken if it meant he would hear Jena laugh.

"I guess I'm kind of used to it. You know, starting at a new school. I mean, I've been doing it all my life. I was like the professional new girl. I could've written a book. But this time was different, because, technically, I did know someone. Kind of." It turns out that the move to Parsons Falls wasn't random. Tilda's mother and Jena's were college roommates and the two had always kept in touch, though the families had never met. Mrs. Kopel attended the funeral, and when she heard that the General was planning to retire she suggested he and Jena should move to Parsons Falls. At least they would know someone. "So, as soon as we got here, the Kopels had us over and I met Tilda. We clicked right away." She crumples the chip bag into a ball and drops it on the counter. "And this time's also different because we're staying put. Before I never really made friends or got involved in things because I knew we'd be moving again. But not anymore. That's why I'm really working hard to fit in and belong."

"So is that why you joined the drama club? To meet people and be part of things? Get a whole crew of new friends in one go?"

"Not really. Mainly I joined because of Tilda. I mean, I'm so lucky Tilda likes me and right away wanted to be my friend. I mean, can you imagine if she didn't?"

He has no trouble imagining that.

"I mean, what would I have done?"

If she didn't just not like you but actually disliked you, you would have wished your father had stayed in the army and been stationed at least ten thousand miles away.

"Anyway, Tilda wanted me to do drama. She believes in being out there, you know?" Oh, he knows. She's the girl who could upstage the corpse at a funeral. "Of course, she's a terrific actor and I'm not. I didn't even get a nonspeaking part, that's how bad I am. I'm a stagehand." She passes him the bowl of pretzels. "But I'm glad I let her talk me into it. Because I never realized before how really amazing acting is. And it's a really fun play. They haven't started rehearsals yet, but I've been helping Tilda learn her lines and I really envy her. You know, because, even if it's only for a little while, it must be such a relief to be someone else for a change."

How many times has he wished he was someone else? Not with a different family or anything like that. And he'd still love his music and be good at math and have the same friends and a large gray cat with a bent ear named Charley Patton who loves blueberry jam, but he'd be different. Socially confident. Always sure of himself. Never gawky, graceless, or the object of peer disapproval. Better-looking. Taller.

The story goes that the great bluesman Robert Johnson met the Devil at a crossroads and sold his soul in exchange for his legendary musical gift.

Josh Shine is at a crossroads of his own at this moment as he and Jena stand together in the Capistranos' kitchen. He can ignore what she just said about what a relief it must be to be someone else. Or he can see it as a connection to her that he never hoped for. A much deeper connection than liking the same music. *She's just like me.*

He chooses not to ignore it.

Friends

Sunday morning is bright and clear, and Josh's mood is just as sunny. This is the happiest he's felt in weeks—since he first saw Jenevieve Capistrano and started to realize that the guitar was not going to be his only passion. He and Jena watched two movies together last night—flopped side by side on the couch with the snack bowls between them—talking and laughing as if it was something they did every week. He can't stop thinking about it. They might even have gone for a triple-header, but the General came home and, without actually saying anything more than *Getting late, isn't it?*, threw Josh out.

Now, doing something he does do every week, Josh leaves the yoga center with Ramona. Ramona, who also can't stop thinking about last night, is unusually quiet. If Josh is a day of blue skies and sunshine, Ramona is overcast, gray and deciding whether to rain or not. Josh doesn't notice. He's too busy telling her about his latest disagreement with Mr. Burleigh. Mr. Burleigh is taking the class to see a play in the new year, and Josh suggested that instead of a standard performance they go to a production by the National Theatre of the Deaf. "I just think it would be a more powerful and significant experience," Josh is saying as they cross the street to the Laughing Moon. Ramona nods. "There are whole other experiences that we never think about," says Josh. "Nobody in the class even knew there is a National Theatre of the Deaf. I think that's pretty sad."

Ramona says, "Um," and opens the door. It isn't until they get their drinks and find a table that Ramona finally speaks.

She looks at him as he gets ready to sit and says in her I-don't-play-games way, "So what's going on with you and the army brat?"

Tea sloshes over the rim of his cup as he sets it down. "What?" He wasn't expecting this.

"I saw you go into her house last night." Her gaze is steady as a boulder. "So, you know, I was wondering."

Though, given his views on the ironic nature of life, maybe he should have been expecting this. It probably wouldn't matter what time he'd gone over to Jena's—or if there was a hurricane and he'd crawled up the street on his stomach with a sombrero on his head—at the exact moment he reached the Capistranos', Ramona would have been looking out the window and seen him.

He tries to make a joke of it. "Ramona Minamoto, were you spying on me?" *Ha ha ha*.

She doesn't laugh. "If I was spying on you I'd've been outside the Salcedos', where you usually are on Saturday nights. And not in my house, where I usually am." She does, however, smile: an exaggerated, say-cheese grin. "Anyway, I could be wrong, but Jena doesn't seem like the chess club type to me. Does that mean she joined the band?"

He doesn't know what she's talking about. Who mentioned the band or the chess club? "What?"

Ramona shakes her teabag over her cup before dropping it onto her saucer. "Sal said you bailed from movie night and he thought it was because of either the band or the club. So I was wondering which Jena joined."

Ah. So that's who mentioned them. Sal, the master of communication. He should probably have known that, too.

"Well, Sal was wrong, and you're not funny." He mops up the spilled tea with his napkin.

"You still haven't answered my question." No one has ever accused Mo of giving up easily. "What's going on with you and Jena?"

"Nothing's going on. We're friends."

"Really?" She looks back at him as if she has telepathic vision, straight into his devious mind. "I thought you said she was just someone in your class. I didn't realize you'd become friends." Making it sound as if she just found out that he'd joined a cult.

"Well, we have." He puts both his hands around his cup. "And, not that it's any of your or Sal's business, but her dad was going out and she doesn't like to be alone at night so I said I'd keep her company."

Ramona comes close enough to scowling to make it obvious that she isn't impressed by his altruism. She knows it isn't any of her business. Not really. He can do what he wants. But still. "So how come you got to be the cavalry? What happened to Tilda and her other pals? They all get sucked into the vortex?"

"I don't know what happened to Tilda," Josh lies. "Jena asked me over and I said yes because I felt sorry for her. She really hates being alone. I don't know why you're making a big deal out of it."

"I'm not." She shrugs. Nonchalantly. Exactly as if she hasn't been making a big deal of it. "I was just kind of curious. You didn't mention that was why she wanted your number. You said it was about homework."

And when did Ramona decide that she doesn't want

to be a costume designer, she wants to be a prosecuting attorney?

"Have I been taken in for questioning or something? Have you started working for the CIA?"

She laughs. "You know me. I'm antiestablishment, but I do have an inquiring mind."

Josh laughs, too. Maybe they are just joking around. "You mean, you're really nosy."

"That too." Ramona's smile is like a hug. "It's just . . . you know . . . you're my friend . . . I like to know what's going on."

"I told you, nothing's going on." His smile is like a nudge. "Get real, Mo. Do you think a girl like her would be interested in me?" He opens his arms. "Me? Really?"

She shakes her head. "No. Not in a million centuries." Dishonesty has never been one of Ramona's traits. "I'm surprised she ever started talking to you."

"I was in a tree. You know, the one in front of their house?"

"Oh, in the tree. Of course." *How could I be so dim?* "Now I understand completely."

"That's how we got to be friends. And that's all we are." Which, whether he likes it or not, is true.

Ramona gives him another smile. She really wants to believe him.

* * *

When she saw Josh at the Capistranos', Ramona wondered what Tilda Kopel would think of him and Jena hanging out together, which makes it almost a shame that Ramona is watching a sixties movie with Sal this afternoon and not at the Capistranos' where that important opinion is about to be given.

Because the General is home, Jena and Tilda have gone to her room to change the color of their nail polish and discuss Tilda's date with Anton Chersky. This was their third date, and they are now officially seeing each other. "And this is good news for you, too," Tilda is saying. "Anton has lots of friends who are almost as awesome as he is. We're guaranteed to find someone perfect for you."

"Me?" Jena laughs. "Anton's friends aren't going to be interested in me."

"Of course they are." Tilda has never been burdened by a lack of confidence. "You're my bestie. They'll be interested." She leans back against the pillows. "So what'd you wind up doing last night?" And then, because she can't imagine anything that wouldn't be improved by her presence, adds, "I hope you weren't too bored."

"No, I was fine." Jena picks up her soda from the table next to the bed. "Josh came over and we watched a couple of movies."

Tilda's smile is so constant that it might be painted on like a doll's, but now it slips ever so slightly. A doll that's been left out in the backyard all winter. "Who?"

"Josh," repeats Jena. "You know. Josh Shine? He's in Mr. Burleigh's class?"

"What?" Tilda laughs, a sound reminiscent of a small animal being choked. "Josh Shine? You're kidding, right?"

Jena hasn't yet learned to read every look, gesture, and inflection of Tilda's, and so has no idea that she is about to give the wrong answer. "No. You know I hate being by myself. So he said he'd keep me company."

"Josh Shine." Tilda speaks slowly, one word at a time. "You hung out with Josh Shine last night."

Since it's unlikely that Tilda has suddenly gone deaf or unconscious, Jena sits up a little straighter. "And? What's wrong with that?"

"Oh, nothing." Tilda stares back at her, wide-eyed and innocent-looking as Bambi. "If you don't mind hanging out with weirdos."

"Weirdos?" If Jena sits up any straighter she'll be standing. Tilda has rolled her eyes or made a give-me-a-break face when Josh said something outrageous in class, but until this moment Jena had no idea that on Tilda's personal popularity list Joshua Shine might well be somewhere below boiled cabbage and pleated skirts.

"Josh isn't weird." Under the isn't-he? gaze of her best friend in the world, Jena shifts uncomfortably. "I mean, he's a little different—he's not like Anton. . . ." Anton is the high-school-hero type. "But he's not weird."

"Isn't he?" Tilda asks this as if she is genuinely interested in what Jena has to say, and not about to answer her question herself. Nevertheless, before Jena can manage even a quick *No, he isn't*, Tilda launches into a long list of Joshua Shine's aberrant behavior that begins in elementary school and marches resolutely into high school. "And I don't know if you know it or not," says Tilda, "but last year he tried to get the Christmas dance canceled!"

This is something Jena didn't know. "He did? Really? But why?"

"Yes, really. How bizarre is that? And don't ask me why. I don't have a twisted mind like that. Maybe because he couldn't get a date—I mean, who would go out with him?—so he didn't want anybody else to have fun."

"Oh, that doesn't sou—"

"Whatever." Tilda waves Jena's doubts away. "He's always coming up with bizarre ideas like that. What about his latest brainwave? I mean, come on. You can't believe that's something a normal person would think of. Instead of going to see a regular play, we should go to one for deaf people?"

Mr. Burleigh's reaction to Josh's suggestion (*I think we should stick to the original plan, Mr. Shine*) was mild compared to Tilda's.

"I think he figured it'd be interesting," defends Jena. "You know, broaden our horizons. And anyway, I thought he said it's not just in sign language. There's speaking, too." Jena didn't think it was as bad an idea as some people. Though this is not an opinion she expressed before, and not one she is planning to express now.

"Whatever." Tilda dismisses this with another wave. "Thank God Mr. Burleigh vetoed it. Even some boring Shakespeare play's better than that." She takes her own soda from the table on her side of the bed. "So what about the Pod Squad? Did they come over, too?"

"The Pod Squad?" repeats Jena.

"It's what everybody used to call Josh, Carver, and Sal." Tilda explains about the debate in eighth grade. "It's not just Shine. His friends are just as weird as he is. I know you know Sal from the drama club, but have you ever met Carver? All he ever talks about is how the world is coming to an end because we're destroying everything."

"Well, lots of people agree with him." Jena isn't arguing so much as mentioning. "Not my dad; the General says it's all crap, but lots of scientists and—"

"Get real, Jen," orders Tilda. "I mean, look around you." She waves toward the window. "Does it look like the end of the world?"

"Well, no, I guess—"

"Of course it doesn't. It's exactly how it's always been. Only better. And what about Carver blowing up the science lab? You don't think that's seriously strange?"

"I thought it was an accident."

"That's their story." One that Tilda doesn't seem to believe.

"Sal's not weird like that," says Jena. "I know he's pretty intense and kind of hyper, but you said Mr. Boxhill thinks Sal's, like, some kind of genius."

Mr. Boxhill did say that, and Tilda did repeat it. But there is no positive quality that can't be made negative in the right hands.

"It's a known fact that people who are really smart can be crazy," Tilda tells her. "And if you ask me, that describes the three of them. I mean, what about that documentary Sal and Josh made last year? What about that?"

Here is something else of which Jena wasn't aware.

"That's no surprise," says Tilda. "Everybody wants to forget it. The two of them went around asking people stupid questions just to embarrass them."

"People?" echoes Jena. "You mean at school?"

"Yes, at school." Sal was writer, cameraman, and director. Josh was the interviewer. They randomly stopped students to ask them questions about current world events, geography, and history. "And then they actually showed this dumb movie in assembly. Like it was some big joke." Some interviews were funnier than others, of course; Tilda's got quite a few laughs, her knowledge of current world events, geography, and history being considerably less than her knowledge of fashion, popular movies, and music. "I don't know why the principal let them show it. And God knows why I let them con me into being interviewed. I know they're nuts. But they made it sound like it was going to be a survey, you know? Like 'what's your favorite lipstick' and 'what movie star would you like most to date'. Stuff like that. Instead it was all stuff like 'who's the president of Canada' and 'can you find Cameroon on a map.' Like anybody's even heard of Cameroon! If that's not insane I'd like to know what is."

Is Josh crazy? wonders Jena. *Is that why he's so different?* "I guess . . ."

"It's, like, totally true." Tilda leans toward Jena so their shoulders touch. "Anyway, I wasn't being judgmental or anything. I was just saying what everybody else thinks. If you want to go out with Josh Shine, that's your business. Don't let me influence you. I won't say another word."

"Oh, it's nothing like that," Jena quickly assures her. "I'm not interested in him like that. We're just friends."

"Well, that's all cool," says Tilda. "So long as you're sure."

Jena nods. "Oh, I'm sure."

If she wasn't before, she definitely is now.

Zugzwanged

So now Josh and Jena are friends.

Not friends like Jena and Tilda, of course. Tilda is Jena's official best friend. She sleeps over and shares secrets, cosmetics, and clothes. Tilda's the friend who discusses things like sex, periods, and breast implants with Jena. If they were flowers they'd both be roses. Not only do they look as if they belong together, when they are together they never stop talking, and when they aren't together they message and text all the time. As if even an hour with no communication between them would end life as we know it.

And not friends like the other kids who make up Jena's social life—Tilda's crowd—the movies-pizza-bowling-party crew. The kids who make teenagedom look cool and fun.

Josh has nothing to do with Tilda or her crowd.

Which breaks no hearts on either side. Despite that, he has grown as close to Jena as it's possible to get without being either her boyfriend, a relative, or Tilda Kopel. He's the friend whose clothes Jena wouldn't want to borrow, who would undoubtedly be shot by her father if he even thought of staying overnight and who would rather have a mouse ear grafted to the top of his head than get involved in a conversation about sex, blood, or breasts with anyone, especially Jenevieve Capistrano. He's the friend who never hangs out with her and her crowd on weekends—the mainly indoors, private, at-home friend (though because of Ramona's tendency to look out her window, the home is as often his as Jena's). The one who is always available, even at short notice, to run errands, watch a movie, or help with homework. Or just be there when no one else is around.

Being a human isn't easy. Give a dog a bowl of food and a pat on the head, and he'll be wagging his tail. Give a cat your chair by the fire and a few treats, and the purring will begin. People, however, are far more complicated. Liable to create problems for themselves or make worse the ones that exist. People are full of contradictions, as straightforward as a maze. As an example of this, Josh should be pretty pleased with things right now—or at least grateful to the kindness of the cosmos. He got what he thought he wanted, and a lot more than he thought he would get. Unofficial backup best friend. Who could have predicted that? Who dared hope?

And is he happy? Does he look up at the sky every night and thank the stars?

No, he isn't. No, he does not. The happiness he felt when they first became friends has faded the closer they've become.

Before that fateful Saturday night, Josh was interested in Jenevieve the way a poor man might be interested in expensive cars—turning his head to look when one passes, occasionally letting out an if-only sigh. Now, however, Josh is officially smitten. *Smitten*—from the verb *smite,* to strike with a hard blow. Smite, smote, smiting, smitten. She couldn't have struck him a harder blow if she'd smashed him over the head with a mallet. The only time Josh ever felt worse than this was when his dad died. He locks himself in his room, playing heartbreak songs about unrequited love (of which there are several thousand more than you might have thought). When he looks at the stars, it isn't because he is sleepless with happiness but with hopelessness—the last thing on his mind is thanking them. For although Jenevieve Capistrano is nothing like the Devil—no horns, no hooves, no tail, and a much nicer nature—Josh feels as though he must be in Hell. If he walks her home after school because Tilda's busy, or goes to the grocery store with her because the Capistranos have run out of the General's favorite cereal, he has to fight the temptation to take her hand as they walk. When it's his turn to choose a movie he always picks something that might scare her enough to grab hold of him. Heads together over a tricky math problem, he smells the peppermint shampoo she uses and wants to put his face in her hair.

And then there was that sudden storm. He'd gone with her to the dentist because she's afraid of the dentist and didn't want to go alone, but Tilda is even more afraid of dentists, so Josh was the default choice. On the way home the sky suddenly went black and it started to rain as if it meant to wash the planet clean. Jena wasn't dressed for bad weather. The day had started mild and sunny, and she was wearing a cotton dress and a sweater. They ducked under a tree for shelter. Josh took off his jacket and draped it over their shoulders and heads, just like in a movie. She was as close to him as skin, so close he was sure she could hear the racket his heart was making. *Do something*, he told himself. *Kiss her.* She was looking at him as if maybe he was going to kiss her—as if maybe she might even kiss him back. Or was she? It would have been a good time to be a boy who acted before he thought, but, of course, Josh isn't that boy. He didn't act; he thought. He thought that her look might not be saying, *Are you going to kiss me?* It might be saying, *I can tell from your breath what you had for lunch.* The moment passed like all the others.

Nonetheless, he is always on the verge of making a move. *Do it!* He urges himself. *Put your arm around her . . . hug her . . . kiss her . . . for God's sake, at least tell her you like her a lot. . . .* But those are things he only does in dreams. Some might compare him to Tantalus. In Greek mythology, the gods punished Tantalus by making him spend eternity in a pool of water that receded every time he tried to take a drink, and underneath a tree that moved out of reach every time he tried to pick a piece of fruit. Josh thinks of himself more as someone standing at the door who can't bring himself to ring the bell.

He doesn't know what to do. Should he tell her how he feels, or should he keep his mouth shut? Should he rock the ship of friends or should he stay seated with his life jacket on, knowing that, if he rocks the ship, there's a high risk of falling into the icy, oceanic waters of used-to-be and drowning?

Josh doesn't know who to talk to. Who can give him useful advice? He trawls through his mother's magazines, but the advice columns don't seem to be covering unrequited adolescent love this season. His father is dead; his mother is out as an option. She's always said that Josh can talk to her about anything, that's what she's here for, but he prefers to think that she's here to make sure he lives to adulthood and knows how to cook and change a metal washer, not act as a consultant on intimate relationships. They've had a few parent-son conversations about sex, girls, and STDs—all of them initiated by her, and all of them embarrassing enough to cause him physical pain. He'd sooner talk to Dr. Wanneski, the school psychologist, and he'd have to be seriously out of his mind to do that. First choice has to be Carver. Not wanting to add to his mother's unhappiness, it was Carver Josh went to when his father's heart gave out in the parking lot of Food World, where he'd stopped for ice cream on his way home from work; Carver who sat up weekend nights watching movies with him and acting as if he didn't notice Josh's tears; Carver who went to the funeral and sat on one side of him, Ramona on the other, each holding one of his hands.

He waits until they're alone. Carver's sisters ensure that the Jefferson house is always filled with noise and activity and teetering on the edge of chaos, but in Carver's room calm and order reign. The only sounds are the classical Spanish guitar music playing softly in the background and the *click-clack* of the counters as Carver lays out his pieces on the backgammon board.

"I have something I need to talk to you about," says Josh to the top of Carver's head.

Carver looks up, curious. "What is it?"

"It's nothing really. It's . . ." Josh gazes at the board. "It's just . . ." He straightens one of his rows.

Carver gives the table a shake. "For Christ's sake, Joshua, what is it?"

Josh meets his eyes. "There's this girl—"

"I knew it!" crows Carver. "I told Sal something was going on. You've become very unreliable lately."

"I have?" This is news to him.

"Yes, you have. Something's always coming up at the last minute."

"Always?" It isn't always; Jena has a busy social life. It's barely sometimes. "I think that's an exaggeration."

"Okay, maybe not always," Carver concedes, "but a hell of a lot more than it used to. The only time I remember you ditching movie night at the last minute was when you got that bug and started projectile vomiting. But this fall you've bailed a couple of times." He winks. "Not that anybody's counting."

"And what'd Sal say?" Sal's been talking to Ramona; has Ramona been talking to Sal?

Carver grins. "Oh, he agreed. But Sal never bought your 'this is just in general' crap. He always thought it was about a girl." It's a Cheshire-cat grin. "So who are we talking about here? Is it anyone I know?"

"No, it isn't anyone you know." So far he hasn't told anyone about his friendship with Jena. Ramona knows, but she obviously hasn't said anything either. "It's just this girl I kind of, you know, like."

"Right." Carver taps a checker against the edge of the board. "This girl you kind of, you know, like." He looks at Josh as if he's checking a water sample for pollution. "But you won't tell me who it is. Can I guess?"

"You don't have to guess. It's not important. I'm just not sure what to do, that's all." He turns back to laying pieces on a point. "What if it was you? What would you do?"

"I'd ask her out."

"But that's the thing. I can't just ask her out."

"Can't? Why not?" Carver looks as if he can't decide if he's bewildered or simply amused. "You mean because you don't speak the same language, you don't actually know her, she's just some girl you saw in a movie, or because she has a boyfriend who could make you wish you'd been born a serf in the Middle Ages?"

"She's not seeing anybody—obviously, I wouldn't even think of asking her out if she was seeing somebody.

I'm just really afraid I don't stand the chance of a baby turtle in a major oil spill with her."

"Why not?"

"What do you mean 'why not?'"

"Why do you think you don't stand a chance? Do you know she doesn't like you? Did she tell everyone in sixth grade that you cheated on a test?" That would be Tilda Kopel because she was jealous that Carver had his picture in the paper for winning first prize in the statewide science fair. Nobody believed her—everyone knew how smart he is—which made her like Carver even less. "Did she try to drown you?" That was at the class picnic in seventh grade. Carver was going on about the toxic chemicals in makeup and Olivia Fenster dumped a glass of juice over his head. Carver's track record with girls is poor; maybe he was the wrong person to confide in.

"No, nothing like that," Josh assures him. "I am friends with this girl. I know she likes me. And so far she hasn't tried to humiliate or physically hurt me. But I can't get up the nerve to say anything."

"Irrational terror," says Carver. "Fear of the unknown. But if you're friends—"

"Absolutely. We're friends. But I don't know how to move to the next level. Or if I should. I mean, maybe there isn't a next level. This may be as far as it goes."

Carver glances at the white disc in his hand. "Right. So you're friends with this girl but you can't ask her out." He sets down the piece and looks up. "I'm sorry, but I truly don't see the problem. You already have your foot in the door."

"But what if she doesn't *like me* like me? What if she breaks my foot slamming the door in my face?"

"Ah, I get it. Shit-scared of rejection." He fingers another checker. "So ask her. End the suspense."

Everything is easier when the problem isn't yours.

"Okay. But one of the things is that this girl is really attractive. All the guys notice her. She's a standout."

"Right. Really attractive." Carver's mouth doesn't move, but he manages to look as if he's chewing something. Slowly. "Kind of like, say, Ramona? Really attractive like that?"

"Ramona?" How did Ramona get into this conversation? "No, not like her at all. Guys notice Ramona because she's taller than most of them."

Now Carver only looks amused. "I don't think that's the only reason, Josh. Ramona—"

"No, I know. She's got that mouth and those eyebrows."

"So this girl's not—she's nothing like Ramona. But she's attractive." Carver still seems to be chewing. "More attractive than you."

As if that might be hard.

"Exactly. Way more attractive than I am."

Carver makes a don't-sweat-it face. "You're overthinking this. Girls aren't like guys. They don't have penises so they think more with their brains than we do. You're always seeing knockout women with men who look like frogs."

Josh doesn't have to look far for proof that Carver's right. In the family photograph on the mantelpiece in the living room, his mother looks like she might once have been a model, but the best you can say about his dad is that at least he looks as if he once had hair. "Okay, we'll skip the looks gap. What about the social hierarchy chasm? Let's say that if we were in seventeenth-century Europe this girl would belong to the aristocracy and I'd be mucking out the stables."

"Ah," says Carver. "Different leagues. The tyranny of the societal pecking order." He shrugs. "But, still, there is a friendship. Abysses have been crossed. Commoners have married kings."

"No abysses have been crossed with her other friends. I'm not part of her social scene."

He shrugs again. "There's only one way to find out if you stand a chance. She can only say no."

Which isn't true, of course. She could laugh her heart out and run into the hills.

"She might be so thrown that she doesn't even want to be just friends anymore. So I'd lose what I have." Josh picks up the dice. "You see the problem now? I'm zugzwanged."

Carver rolls his eyes. "And what does *zugzwanged* mean in the world of Joshua Shine?"

"It's a chess term. It's when you're forced to move, but any move you take will make things worse for you. What I'm saying is, if I tell her and she doesn't feel like that about me, she may never speak to me again."

"But if you don't say anything and she does feel like that, she'll never know how you feel and will wind up dating some good-looking, super slick guy—but always be haunted by the thought that there's something missing from her life and never know what."

"Exactly," says Josh.

"On the other hand, what if you tell her and she says she's been waiting for you to confess your love? Then it's all flowers falling out of the sky and guys in puffy shirts playing violins."

"But if she doesn't, I might end up not even having her as a friend."

"Right," says Carver. "So, basically, you're right on the horns of a dilemma here. Damned if you do, and damned if you don't."

"That's what I said," says Josh. "I'm totally zugzwanged."

"Ergo, one might as well go for it. You don't want to do a Hamlet, going back and forth about what to do, and doing sweet nothing."

This is undoubtedly the only time anyone will compare Josh to a Shakespeare character that isn't an elf.

"Maybe . . ."

"One more question." Carver folds his arms on the edge of the table and leans toward him. "Since it isn't . . . Are we talking about the girl with the My Little Pony hair? Is that who we're talking about?"

"It's not pink anymore," says Josh.

"It is in the eye of my mind." Carver is shaking his head. "Shit, man," says Carver. "Capistrano. It didn't occur to—I think I've changed my opinion. She's part of Clan Kopel, brother. There's no way she'd ever go out with you. You're not in the same league. You're not even playing the same game."

They All Asked About You

"Hey! Wait up! You going my way?"

Jena, hurrying through the rain with her book bag over her head, stops and turns around. Behind her, like a lighthouse on a dark and stormy night, is Ramona Minamoto in a bright yellow slicker, over her head an oiled-paper Chinese umbrella decorated with dragons.

"Oh, hi," says Jena. "I'm on my way home."

"Me, too." Ramona strides toward her. "Get under."

"Oh, no. It's okay. I'm—"

"Getting soaked," finishes Ramona.

"I'm fine. Really." Mesmerizing as the sight of Ramona is, Jena's eyes dart around her.

Ramona laughs. "It's okay. Nobody's going to see you. Tilda's in rehearsal."

Jena has heard a lot about Ramona from Tilda, none of it good. Tilda may not have a high opinion of Josh, but her opinion of Ramona is low enough to hit oil. Ramona, according to Tilda, is an infected boil on the butt of life. Stuck up. Peculiar. Sarcastic. Has a major attitude problem. Never knows when to keep her mouth shut. What Tilda didn't mention is that Ramona can read minds.

"Oh, Tilda wouldn't—" Yes, she would. There's no way she'd stand for Jena being chummy with Ramona.

"I was just kidding." Ramona slides the umbrella over Jena.

Jena could say she just remembered she has to go into town for something. It isn't just Tilda who doesn't like Ramona. The General has assessed his new neighbors and found them far below his standards. He's noted Mrs. Minamoto's flamboyant clothes and Mr. Minamoto's necklaces and clogs—and their only child, of course, who manages to combine her parents' unconventionality and add something to it of her own. The only good thing he has to say about them is that at least they're capitalists. Serious capitalists. He's seen the prices in their store. But, in what Josh would say is an example of what he means by life's many ironies, the fact that her father, Tilda, and her other friends would disapprove of her fraternizing with Ramona makes Jena want to. She can just picture their faces. That alone makes her feel like a person who doesn't always do as she's told. And, since her father's at work and Tilda's rehearsing, Jena falls into step beside Ramona.

"So how are you liking Parsons Falls?" asks Ramona as they walk through the downpour under the warm, patterned light of the Chinese umbrella.

Jena likes it a lot. It's a great town. The school's really good. And she's already made so many friends. She gives Ramona a sideways glance. "I know you and Tilda—"

Hate each other are the words she can't quite bring herself to say.

"Hey, it's cool," Ramona assures her. "You know that old saying: different strokes for different folks."

Jena, who didn't, nods.

"Think how boring the world would be if everybody was exactly the same and liked all the same people and things," Ramona goes on. "I mean, God . . . talk about land of the zombies . . ."

Jena laughs—a sound that doesn't come even close to making Ramona think of hot-fudge sauce. "You know, you're right. I guess I never thought of it like that."

They talk about the play, and Sal, and then, as they stop on their street between their houses, Jena mentions Josh. "So you and Josh are really good friends," she says.

"Yeah," says Ramona. "Ever since we were kids."

"That must be cool. Knowing somebody for so long."

Jena shifts from one foot to the other. "He's a nice guy."

Ramona agrees. "The best."

"I . . . You . . ." If she fidgets any more she'll be dancing. "At first I thought you two must be a couple."

Ramona smiles. "Is that a question?"

"No. Oh, no. Josh said you're just friends." Jena's laugh can't decide whether it's nervous or embarrassed. "I've never really had a boy for a friend before. You know, not since grade school. I kind of didn't think it was possible. Not really. But now that I'm friends with Josh I get it. It's just, you know, you're both kind of—kind of unusual." Adding quickly, "I don't mean that in a bad way. It's just that it seemed obvious you'd be together."

Not to everybody it isn't, thinks Ramona. But what she says is, "Sorry to disappoint you, but we're just friends."

"So. I hear you have a thing for the new girl in town." The last time Sal looked this happy was when he got his state-of-the-art video camera.

"I'll take a wild guess," says Josh. "You've been talking to Carver."

"We're your friends. We're interested in your happiness."

That and they both have big mouths.

"So that's what you're doing when you dump us?" Sal

makes a what-a-dope-I-am face. "And I thought—but you were hanging out with what's-her-name." He laughs. "You kept that pretty quiet."

"Wouldn't you?" counters Josh. "I'm not exactly in her crowd."

"Put another way, she's not in yours." Sal cocks his head to one side, as if trying to see Josh from a different angle. "So what did you decide? You going to ask her out?"

"I don't know. Carver thinks I shouldn't."

"What does Carver know? He's not normal. You heard him, he doesn't even believe in girls."

"Maybe because he doesn't think girls believe in him."

"Exactly. He's passing on his negativity to you. I think you should ask her out." He punches Josh in the arm. "Think of it as an adventure. You'll be the first to boldly go where none of us has gone before."

"What if I encounter hostile aliens and end up in a zoo in a distant galaxy and I spend the rest of my life wishing I'd never left home?"

"What if you don't?" asks Sal.

After Carver, the person Josh has shared the most pain and humiliation with over the years is Ramona. Not only does she know him as well as anyone could without actually being able to read his mind, she has the added advantage of being a girl. A point of view he could probably use right now. Guys may be able to build computers and spaceships and microwave ovens, but Josh isn't convinced they know much about how the female brain works. It's a foreign country with different rules and a dangerous terrain. He needs a guide.

Ramona stares at him for at least five solid seconds before she says anything, and then she says, "What?" For just a second she looks so pale she might almost be wearing kabuki makeup.

It's Sunday morning, and they're having their after-class tea. He figured it was best to have this conversation when she's relaxed, at one with her body and at peace with the world—rather than when she's in a mood to kick the world in the head.

"I was just wondering, you know." He carefully scoops the teabag from his cup so he doesn't have to look at the expression of shock on her face. Or possibly horror. She doesn't seem to be as mellow as he'd hoped.

"Let me get this straight." She's still wearing the blue tank top she wore for yoga and has her hair tied back, so that she reminds him of Lara Croft in taking-care-of-business mode. Especially since she looks as if she's pointing pistols at him. "You were wondering if *I've* ever been interested in anyone?"

He thought it would be better to take the back road into this conversation. It seems to him that, Olivia Fenster aside, in a situation where a guy will hit you (or throw the nearest glass of liquid over your head) most girls will come up with something much more subtle, so he's trying to be subtle. But maybe he was wrong.

"Why were you wondering that?"

For God's sake. It's not as if he said he was wondering if she wears boxers or secretly eats dog biscuits. What's so strange about wondering if she's ever liked someone?

"I just was." He gives her what he hopes is a disarming smile. "I'm not asking you to name names, Mo. I was just curious, that's all. It's not a ridiculous suggestion. You are, you know . . . attractive."

"I am?"

This is what he means about girls. He can't tell whether she's pleased that he noticed, or if she thinks he has an ulterior motive for mentioning it.

"Yeah." Best not to say anything about the eyebrows or the mouth.

"You think I'm attractive?"

Did she emphasize *you* or *attractive*? She isn't getting the wrong idea, is she? He doesn't want her to get the wrong idea. Ramona is someone who wouldn't hesitate to laugh her heart out at him: *What the hell? You like me? Are you on drugs?*

"It's not just me," Josh assures her. "Lots of people think so."

"Oh." Her expression and tone are the same, but something's changed. It's as if someone opened the door. It seems that it may be snowing outside. Very heavily. "Right. Lots of people."

"So?" he prods. "Anything? A secret passion? A fleeting infatuation? Some schoolgirl crush?"

"No. Nothing." She picks up a sugar packet. "Have you checked out the boys in our school, Joshua? Most of them are all about contact sports and food fights. Who would I be interested in?" She whacks the sugar against the table. "One of the teachers? Maybe Break-'em-down Burleigh? Yeah, he's perfect. Not just because of his winning personality but because he has a wife and two children, too. He's practically irresistible. And think of the scandal! We'd hit all the tabloids and go viral. That's all I've ever wanted out of life."

"Okay. Okay. I'm sorry. I was just curious, that's all. You know. Because you are attractive and I've never known you to date or anything."

"That's because I haven't." This is one of the few times she's ever reminded him of her mother; she looks like she's trying to commune with the spirits of the woodland. And convince them to make him disappear. "Neither have you dated or anything." She gives the bag of sugar another whack. "Unless you've been holding out on me."

"My only 'anything' was the time I walked Briony Shaksi to her house because there was a cat at the corner of her street she was afraid of." Briony never thanked him and never spoke to him again; the cat attacked him. "But I'm not attractive. Expectations are way lower for someone like me."

Ramona is not a girl to blush, but she blushes now. "Are they?"

"Yes, they are."

"Well, I haven't. Been interested in anyone." Of course, she is not a girl to mumble, either. "Not really."

Not really. "What does that mean?"

"It means not really. Like maybe when I was really little. Not really."

"Right." Josh nods as if he's thinking that over, when in fact he spent at least an hour last night preparing what he was going to say. "Okay. But let's say you were. Interested in someone. Just supposing. Hypothetically." Her attention is on her tea as she starts to open the packet. "Would you say something, or would you wait for him to make the first move?"

A fine spray of sugar falls on the table.

"Damn!" She brushes it into a tiny pile and reaches for another. "I'm sorry. What did you say?"

He repeats the question.

This time she manages to get the sugar into her cup. "I'd wait for . . . for the other person. You know." She looks into his glasses. "So I didn't make a fool of myself."

"Of course. I agree. That makes perfect sense." He makes a fool of himself enough unintentionally without doing it on purpose. "Only, what if he's waiting for you to say something? What if he's as nervous as you are? Guys don't like rejection any more than girls do."

Possibly less, given the number of men who harm the woman who breaks up with them. But he's not about to mention that now, either; Ramona has a lot to say about male violence.

"Okay, so I do know lots of people are really shy in that kind of situation. Not everybody thinks they're God's gift or knows how to schmooze." She tilts her head so that she seems to be studying his chin. "So I guess I can imagine I might like somebody like that. But I'm like that, too. So how would I know someone wants to go out with me if they keep it a secret?"

"Okay. But how's he going to know that you'd go out with him if *you* keep it a secret? Especially if he's not"—he wonders if he's said too much, but it's too late now—"not experienced with girls."

Ramona takes a sip of tea. "There are signs."

"There are?" Obvious? Subtle? Written in a code no man has ever deciphered? "What kind of signs?"

She gazes into her cup as if the answer is in there. "You know. Signs."

This is what he means about the workings of the female mind. Would he be asking if he knew?

"Yeah, but are they recognizable signs? Or do you need a degree in cryptology to read them?"

She makes a face. If she were Lara Croft she would probably shoot him. "You know if somebody likes you, don't you? Like if they don't run in the opposite direction the second they see you. And they get your jokes. And they have no trouble talking to you."

"Yeah, but there's like, and there's *like*. And don't pretend you don't know what I mean. You're the one who said you wouldn't make the first move."

"Hints." The cup clatters back in its saucer. "I think if someone's interested in someone, they'll be able to tell if the other person's interested in them. You just have to pay attention."

"Right." Josh nods. "I see. Just pay attention."

He still doesn't know to what.

She leans forward, elbows on the table. "So who are we talking about here? Who is it you're interested in?"

"I wasn't talking about me. I was just talking in general."

She makes a yeah-sure face. "It's Capistrano, isn't it? I know you go over there. It has to be her."

"I go over there because we're friends," says Josh. "That's all we are. Just friends."

"And we're friends, too, right?"

"You have to ask?"

"It's just that . . . I don't want you to take this wrong . . ." She seems to be choosing her words from the bottom of a very deep box. "And I don't want to sound mean or anything—but I really don't think that girl is for you, Josh. I'm not saying she's not nice or pretty or anything. But you see the crowd she hangs out with. I know she likes you, but, trust me, you are not her type. Not for a boyfriend."

This is why people have friends. For support and encouragement.

"Then it's lucky I'm not interested in her, isn't it?" says Josh.

"It sure is," says Ramona. "Because Tilda Kopel would never allow it."

Never Make Your Move Too Soon

Josh asked his friends for their advice, and they gave it. Two to one in favor of keeping his mouth shut. Sal with his big-screen dreams obviously has a romantic streak missing in the more pragmatic Carver and Ramona. Put another way, Sal is less realistic, given to fantasy and special effects. So Josh has decided to listen to reason—the foundation on which man's knowledge of the universe is based—and reason says that no best friend of Tilda Kopel will ever be a girlfriend of his. His mouth is shut. Shut, bolted, and double-locked.

Not that he would have much chance to open it. Suddenly, he and Jena are both very busy. Josh has rehearsals with the band; she has to help Tilda with her lines. Josh has a chess match; Jena's busy on the weekend. He sees her at school, of course, and even walks with her after language arts, but always on her other side is that most unlikely (and most efficient) of chaperones, Tilda Kopel in her knee-high boots, short skirts, and force-field smile, acting as if he isn't there, keeping up everyone's end of the conversation and making sure the only words Josh gets to speak concern hello and good-bye.

And then one afternoon he winds up leaving the school grounds with them. After an enthusiastic greeting from Jena and the nod of a queen acknowledging the presence of a very minor servant, Josh walks beside them in silence. Tilda's voice, of course, is the voice heard most. *Blah blah blah, yada yada yada, yakaty yak.* Josh's mind wanders, trying to remember the lyrics to a Joe Jones song about someone who talks too much, when he hears Tilda say, "Let's hope the guy you're seeing Friday night turns out better than that last wastoid. Like, ohmy-God, he was just so not right. I told you that. Didn't I say he had 'vacant space' written all over him?"

Josh doesn't look over at them, but if he were a cat his ears would be standing at attention.

"He wasn't that bad." Jena laughs. "He was a lot better than the guy I went out with before him."

Before him? When did she start dating? How many guys have there been?

"And I know you're right about him, but he wasn't all bad. He was kind of cute."

"You can do much better," Tilda decrees. Jena makes a noncommittal sound that could be agreement or could be doubt. "Trust me," orders Tilda. "Nobody thought he was good enough for you."

"Really?"

"Really," says Tilda.

Jena, it seems, can't argue with Nobody.

Slightly stunned that he's been in Parsons Falls all his life and has never had a single date, but Jena, here since August, has already had at least two, Josh chooses this moment to use one of his opportunities to speak. "See you later," he says. Only Jena shouts after him, "Later!"

She calls him on Saturday afternoon. Tilda was supposed to be spending poker night with Jena, but Tilda is indisposed. "She has really bad cramps," says Jena. "She says it's like she's being squeezed in this giant vise and—"

Josh stops her before blood can become part of the story. "I don't need to know the gruesome details," he assures her. "I'll be over at seven."

Which means he has to adjust his Saturday night plans.

"What are you, rent-a-pal?" asks Sal. "It's a good thing Ramona and Zara are coming along tonight. So at least we won't be a man down."

Ramona? Why is Ramona coming to movie night?

"I asked her," says Sal. "I have a movie she's always wanted to see."

"Really?" Josh can't tell if he's surprised or suspicious—or, possibly, both. "How do you know that?"

"She told me," says Sal.

"And Zara?"

"Carver said she should come, too. You know, since they're friends and usually hang out together on Saturdays."

Thank God no one's going to miss me, thinks Josh.

Nothing is without its drawbacks, of course. Thorns on roses. Seeds in oranges. The challenging shell of the coconut. The drawback to hanging out with Jena at her house is her father. The General makes a habit of answering the door. It may be that he is always the first to greet visitors and salesmen, but Josh takes it personally. The General never stops sizing him up, asking questions he knows Josh either can't answer or will answer incorrectly. That he isn't a fan of Merle Haggard, for example; that he doesn't know how to change a tire; that he has read Howard Zinn's *A People's History of the United States*. When Josh said his mother couldn't recommend a good butcher because they're vegetarians, the General smiled triumphantly. "I should have known."

Tonight Jena answers Josh's knock. He glances into the living room, but there is no large man in a baseball cap looming behind like the threat of nuclear disaster looming over the world.

"It's okay." Jena shuts the door behind him. "Dad already left."

"Really?" Josh follows her along the hallway and into the kitchen to get the snacks. "Does this mean he's decided to accept me?"

Jena laughs. "Not exactly." Her back is to him as she takes something from the counter. "What he's decided is that his daughter is safe with you."

"Because he finally realized what a nice kid I am?"

She turns around, holding two plastic bowls and wearing a smile admirers of the painter Leonardo da Vinci would recognize. "Because he thinks you're probably gay."

"Damn it." He knew the General's small talk was all trick questions. "It's because I'm not into football, isn't it? And because I don't eat dead animals."

"Don't be ridiculous. He's not from the Stone Age. He knows you don't have to be gay to be vegetarian." She hands him one of the bowls. "It's because you're so different from what he thinks is a normal guy." She opens the fridge and takes out a bottle of soda and a bottle of water. "And so that's the explanation he came up with. If he believed in UFOs he'd think you came from another planet." She hands him the water. "And I didn't even tell him you don't drink Coke."

She orders pizza and they move into the living room.

At least partly to change the subject from his deviant dietary habits and disinterest in competitive contact sports, he braces himself for the worst and asks her how her date went, silently begging that it was less successful than the maiden voyage of the *Titanic*.

"OhmyGod! You won't believe it! It was really bizarre. Tilda couldn't stop laughing when I told her."

Maybe God has moved over to Josh's side. Or at least stopped pitting Himself against him.

"I mean, it was way better than this one guy I went out with who not only finished my hamburger platter for me because I put my fork down for like two seconds but couldn't stop talking about his sailboat. Not for a single minute. By the time the evening was over I felt as if I'd been to China with him on it."

"So what happened this time?"

She giggles, a sound that, it seems, only bothers him when it's made by Tilda Kopel. "We went to a movie."

"That doesn't sound too bad. At least you didn't have to talk about sailing."

"Or listen," says Jena.

Josh is smiling, he's relaxed, he's really interested. He's experiencing a form of schadenfreude; being happy over the misery of others. If she'd had a terrific date he'd be so down he'd be below the earth's surface. "So what was so awful?"

"Well, for openers, as soon as the ads came on, he started singing along with the jingles."

"No way!" He gives her a playful shove.

"Yes, really, Josh. I swear it's true. And loud. Really loud. Not like under his breath or anything. So everybody around us could hear it."

"I don't believe you." As much as he'd like to. "Nobody would act like that on a date. Especially not a first date. He might as well have shown up dressed as a giant rabbit. You're making it up."

"OMG, Shine, I'm not making it up. I swear." Jena mimes cutting an *X* over her chest. "Cross my heart and hope to die. Really and truly. People kept looking over at us. Even though it was dark it was sooo excruciatingly embarrassing. I swear, I wanted to crawl under my seat. A giant rabbit would've been a really big improvement on the crooner. At least people would've thought it must be a publicity stunt for some movie."

He's still not convinced. "So what did you do while he was singing backup? Tap along with your feet?"

She rolls her eyes. "You mean, besides pretend I wasn't really with him? Nothing. What could I do?"

"You mean, you just sat there while he impersonated a soda commercial?"

"Oh God, I didn't know what to do. I guess I figured he'd be more like a regular human once the movie started. I thought maybe he was just bored."

"And was he?" He wants her to say *No. No, he grew horns and started pawing the ground as soon as the ads were over.*

"Except for a couple of times when he was the only one laughing, he was okay. I guess he didn't know the soundtrack music."

The good-friend smile is practically glued on Josh's face. "So does that mean you're going to see him again?"

She shakes her head. "I don't think so. He wasn't awful or anything—not like Sailor Boy. But we didn't really click, you know? We kind of bumped into each other and sat there. Keeping the conversation going was like keeping six balls in the air. You had to concentrate. If you took your eyes off it for half a second it stopped."

"And hit you in the head?"

She leans against him, laughing. "Anyway Tilda said there was no point in giving him a second chance because

I could never take him out with our crowd in case there was music. I mean, can you picture it? Everybody would just crack up."

Even without Tilda's guidance, Jena has admitted that she's a serial dater. The most times she's ever been out with the same guy since she started dating in middle school was twice. There was always some fatal flaw. Boring. Slurped his soda. Chewed his nails. Told really dumb jokes. Or there was something not right. No clicking, just that dull thud. No sparks. Jena said you can't start a fire without a spark. Josh didn't tell her she was wrong.

He raises one eyebrow. "So no good-night kiss then?"

She laughs. "I didn't say that, Josh." Blushing makes her eyes shine more. "I mean, he is really, really good-looking."

Of course he is. Jena's dates may all have something wrong with them, but it is never that they have a face that is best seen from behind. She said she knows it must make her seem shallow, but she can't help it that she's attracted to guys who are handsome. Like some people are attracted to blondes or athletes or Southern accents. "Or short people," put in Josh. "There are millions of girls who won't go out with anyone over five foot four." Jena laughed and punched him in the arm. She thinks it's great that he doesn't have a complex.

"Maybe it's me." Jena frowns. "Do you think it's me, Josh? Am I too picky or demanding or something?" The frown deepens. "Maybe it's because of my dad. You know, because he's kind of a perfectionist. And I'm always trying not to, you know, disappoint him."

"Of course you're not too picky," he assures her. "A girl has to have standards." Though he can think of at least one he wishes she'd lower.

"Yeah, but what if I have too many? What if I end up all by myself when I'm, like, forty? Everybody else will have a partner and I'll be alone microwaving meals for one and talking to my computer. Or to a cat. That's what old ladies nobody wants do, isn't it? They get a cat."

"I think they get, like, at least ten cats," says Josh. "But that isn't going to happen to you."

"You can't be sure. Things don't always work out the way you think they will."

"I am sure," says Josh. "Because if you're alone when you're forty, you can always live with me." He's bound to be on his own. "My cooking's pretty limited to chili and spaghetti, but it should improve by then."

"OhmyGod!" Her shriek is worthy of a lottery win. "That's fantastic! What a genius idea!" She pulls her legs up on the sofa and kneels facing him. "Tilda and I talk about maybe living together someday, but you'd be a way better roommate than her."

And more useful than a cat. Because of the opposable thumbs.

Jena makes an I'm-about-to-say-something-totally-shocking face. "Not to be mean, 'cause you know I love Tilda, but she is controlling. Kind of like my dad. And she really is such a major slob."

"Tilda? But she always looks like it takes her at least an hour to get ready for school."

"It does. Sometimes longer." Jena squeezes his hand. "Swear you won't tell anybody what I'm about to tell you."

Who would he tell? It isn't like his friends lose sleep over the burning issue of whether or not Tilda Kopel leaves dirty underwear under her bed.

"But even though, you know, personally, she always looks totally perfect, her room pretty much looks like a crime scene. You know like in a movie when someone breaks in and is looking for the thumb drive with all the secrets on it and they turn everything upside down?"

Jena's room, however, always looks as if it's ready for inspection—which it probably is.

"That's what happens when you weren't raised by a military man," teases Josh. "No discipline or standards."

"But you weren't raised by a military man, and you're super neat," counters Jena. "Even my dad would be impressed if he saw your room."

"That's because I'm anal-retentive."

"Well, Tilda's the opposite. She doesn't retain anything; she throws it everywhere. And she's useless at anything practical. She drinks instant coffee at home because she can't work the coffeemaker. I mean, really? A coffeemaker? And also, I bet you never argue, either." He argues all the time, just not with Jena. "I've never ever heard you shout. Tilda shouts even when she's not mad. But you're always so laid-back and mellow."

Mellow, but also yellow. He wouldn't dream of shouting at Jena—she might never speak to him again.

"You wouldn't make a mess, and you'd clean up, and you'd always be in a good mood. . . ." She gives herself one of the hugs he'd like to give her. "Seriously. I think it'd be perfect if we were roomies, don't you?"

He nods. Pretty close to perfect. Definitely a very near neighbor.

"And you could do all the guy things, too. Which, believe me, Tilda can't do."

He probably can't do them either.

"The *guy things*? You mean, like punching people and driving too fast?"

She laughs. "No, you . . . I mean, like putting up shelves and fixing stuff."

All the things Josh's mother does. The one time he tried to help when the toilet was leaking he nearly drowned them both.

"And I'd never have to worry that we were going to be interested in the same person. And if I wasn't seeing anybody and I needed a date for a party or something, or wanted someone to watch a movie with, you'd be right there."

Here is his chance to say something about how he really feels about her. He doesn't have to wait for the right moment; this is the right moment. All he has to do is tell her that she's right and her father's wrong, there is no way Jena and he would ever be interested in the same person, because even though he doesn't play football he's very heterosexual and the person he's interested in is her. He could at least drop a hint. Make a joke about the well-known power of propinquity, draw the Euler diagram, play her that Mike Nesmith song. He could warn her she'd have to be careful because he might prove irresistible once she's seen him when he's brushing his teeth. *I use red mouthwash. I look like a vampire, and you know how sexy they are.* Or he could be really bold and say: *But what if we fall in love?*

He does none of those things.

"You make it sound so romantic." He winks roguishly, though she may just think he has something in his eye. "I want to rush out and buy some tools so I can start putting up shelves."

"And you know what else? You always make me laugh! So whenever I got stressed or bummed out you'd be there to cheer me up!" Leaning forward slightly, she grabs his hand again. "It really would be so cool, wouldn't it? Think of how much fun we'd have!"

She is so close he can feel her breath, soft as the beating of a ladybug's wings. But he's pretty sure that the heart he hears pounding, heavy as the footsteps of a giant in a fairy tale, is his. This really is the moment he's been waiting for, dreaming of. All he has to do is gently pull her toward him. All he has to do is shift toward her. Just an inch or two. That's all he has to do. Neither of them moves. The world pauses, holding its breath; the only thing in the house besides them is silence. They sit face-to-face, smiling, eyes on eyes and hands entwined. Is she waiting for something? Is he? All he has to do . . .

But suddenly he hears her telling Tilda Kopel about tonight, just the way she told him about her dud dates. *You think the guy humming in the movie theater was bad? Oh my God, that was nothing. Josh Shine came on to me last night! Can you believe it? I swear, Tilda, I didn't know whether to laugh or cry. . . .* Though in his mind they are both laughing, of course, the tears streaming down their faces, dragging streaks of eyeliner with them. *Where's my phone?* gasps Tilda. *I have to tell the others. . . . I have to tweet about it. . . .* She says she wishes Jena had taken a picture. And they collapse into each other's arms. He tells himself to stop. He's doing a Hamlet. Jena would never do that to him. She would never betray him to Tilda like that. Now's his chance. All he has to do is open his mouth and tell her the truth.

The doorbell rings.

The pizza has arrived.

That's what you get if you don't act when you have the opportunity: margherita with extra cheese.

Talk of the Town

"He did? You're sure?" asks Carver. "Mrs. Shine told Ramona that?"

"Yeah, I'm sure," says Sal. "Josh's mom said he suddenly ran out of the house the other night with half an explanation." The half an explanation was that his friend was locked out. "She figured it wasn't you or me 'cause we would've just come over to wait until someone got home to let us in. She called Mo because she thought it must be her. It didn't occur to her it could be Jena."

"Christ," says Carver. "It's worse than I thought."

"That's not all," says Sal. "He did pretty much the same thing to me last week." Sal's father was sick, and Sal and Josh were going to pick up his prescription at the drugstore. After that, they would go back to Josh's to play their favorite computer game, Pan-Galactic Blues, which combines Sal's desire to be in a sci-fi movie and

Josh's love of tactics. Josh was just about to get in the car when his phone started singing. "Next thing I know I'm driving him to Jena's because there's no one else she can turn to. She backed up the toilet and was hysterical and crying that her father was going to have a fit if he saw the mess. Man, you should've seen Josh. You'd think he was Superman and she was Lois Lane, the way he raced off."

"That's definitely not life as we know it," says Carver. "Usually Josh causes plumbing problems; he doesn't solve them."

"Yeah, but who else would she call?" asks Sal. "Tilda?"

Carver laughs. "Now that's a sight I would pay to see. Tilda Kopel with her arm down the bowl."

"I'm having enough trouble picturing Josh," says Sal.

But when he stops laughing Carver wants to know if Sal thinks they should say something to Josh.

"Say what?" asks Sal.

"That he's getting a little carried away. That maybe he should cool it a little."

"What for? He's enjoying himself. He's crazy about her. There's nothing wrong with that."

"If you ask me, the crucial word in that sentence was 'crazy.'"

"You really are a downer, man," says Sal. "Why can't you be happy for him? He's in love."

"He's in something," says Carver. "But I'm not so sure I'd call it love."

Josh is helping Carver with the music for the video Carver's making for his social science project. It's a montage of images of the damage done to the planet by modern civilization—razed jungles, deserts that once were forests, decapitated mountains, polluted oceans, burning rivers, islands of plastic, devastated cities, dead bodies, both human and non. Carver's calling it "Collateral Damage." They've just started going through it for the second time when Josh's phone begins to play "Keep Your Hands Off Her."

"Don't get it," orders Carver. "Not unless it's Maryam Mirzakhani or Judit Polgár. Anyone else, you're busy. Or your mom. You can answer if it's your mom."

Josh knows who it is, of course, and it isn't the renowned mathematician, the chess grandmaster, or his mother. "It might be something important."

Carver gives him an in-your-dreams look. He knows who it is, too. "It isn't. It's the My Little Pony girl."

Josh doesn't ask how Carver knows that because he's too busy hitting Answer.

Jena sounds as if she's been running. "I'm really sorry," she says in a breathless rush, "but my dad's working late, and there's somebody prowling around outside."

"It could just be the wind. Or the rain. It's raining pretty hard."

"It's not the weather, Josh." He can hear her voice charging with panic. "I heard them. I heard footsteps. The rain doesn't wear shoes. And they even tried the back door. I thought my heart was going to jump out of my mouth."

"Okay," says Josh. "You try to calm down. I'll be there as fast as I can." Rain smashes against the window. He can always swim.

"Thankyouthankyouthankyou," Jena gushes. "I knew I could count on you."

Josh looks up from pocketing his phone to see Carver staring at him with an I-told-you-so face.

"So what's tonight's emergency?" asks Carver.

How does he know about Jena's emergencies?

"This is the age of communication," says Carver. "Information at your fingertips. Everything you wanted to know about absolutely anything at the swipe of a screen."

"Yeah, and Sal never knows when to keep his mouth shut."

"He's not the only one," says Carver. "Your mom told Ramona all about how you went running over when Jena locked herself out of the house."

Does he have no privacy? No secrets? So much for avoiding Snapchat, Instagram, and Twitter. He might as well take out ads.

"My mom told Ramona?" Don't they have anything else to talk about? Have all the crises on the planet been solved? Has the world been made peaceful, fair, and just, and no one told him? If not, surely they'd be better off solving the energy crisis than discussing his business. "Are you sure?"

"Yes, indeedy. Said she's never seen you move so fast. Like a speeding bullet." Superheroes don't hesitate, they just rip off their street clothes and jump right in. "And Ramona told Sal."

Oh, for God's sake.

"*Mo* told Sal? Since when are they besties?"

"I guess since you became the satellite to Planet Jena. And he told me how you dumped him because the Capistranos' toilet backed up." Carver leans forward on his arms. "I thought you were just going to be friends with her."

"We are just friends."

"And yet, here you are, reaching for your jacket. About to run into the dark and stormy night because . . . what happened? Did a lightbulb blow?"

"She thinks somebody's trying to get in."

"And?"

"And I have to go make sure she's okay. She hates being alone. She's scared. She heard something."

"Of course she heard something." Carver's reasonableness can be really irritating. "I can hear it, too. It's called wind and rain."

"I told you, she thinks there's someone trying to get in. She heard someone at the door."

"Then why doesn't she call the cops? What are you going to do? Frighten them away with a recitation of the winning game between Fischer and Spassky in 1972?"

"She just needs some moral support."

"Why can't someone else support her morally? Like Ramona. Doesn't she live nearby? Jesus, the girl's built like a warrior princess. Nobody's going to mess with her." He waves a hand at Josh. Dismissively. "You wouldn't intimidate a moth."

"I'm sorry, Carver. I'll come back as soon as the General gets home."

Carver is giving him a but-if-we-level-the-forest-to-plant-oil-palms-what-happens-to-the-orangutans? look. "Maybe you should've said something to her after all. Get it settled."

"I was going to," admits Josh. "But I lost my nerve."

"Well, maybe you should find it," says Carver. "I've

been thinking. Maybe I was mistaken about her. Why does she always call you every time something goes wrong? It's not like there aren't any guys at school who'd be happy to rush over to help her when she gets locked out of the house. She can take her pick of saviors. But she picks you. Why is that?"

"Because I'm her friend."

Carver's face is a question. "Or . . ."

Is this what Ramona meant by signs? Are Jena's cries for help her way of letting him know that she *likes him* likes him?

"You really think maybe I have a chance?"

"Not really. Logic's against it," says Carver. "But stranger things have happened."

Opportunity Lost

The night is dark despite Thomas Edison's best efforts, the wind is trying to knock down everything that stands, and it's raining so hard it does feel like he's swimming. Nonetheless, even Batman wouldn't have reached the Capistranos' much faster, not if he'd had to walk. Every light is on in the house. Josh stands at the foot of the front pathway for a few seconds, trying to figure out what seems odd. And then he realizes: the house is bright as a perigee moon, but it's also just as silent. When Jena's home alone she always has at least one TV blaring, the sound system playing, and the radio on in the kitchen. Minimum. You can always hear the racket from the sidewalk—as if there's a party going on or at least a full house. But not tonight. Tonight she's probably holding her breath.

The door opens even before he reaches it.

"Oh, I'm so glad to see you!" Jena darts onto the porch, grabs his hand and yanks him inside. "I've been so scared I was going to hide in the attic, but then I figured I wouldn't hear the door." The hand that isn't gripping his like a vise has a tight hold on a golf club.

"It's okay. I'm here now." Defending truth, justice, and the American way.

"I knew you'd come." She goes to hug him and whacks him in the calf with the club.

He takes a precautionary step away from her. "Maybe you should put that thing down."

"You don't think we should take it with us? Just in case?"

With them? In case of what?

"Are we going somewhere?"

They're going to investigate. Now that he's here, she's apparently over the worst of her fear and ready to play cop. The kind that carries irons, not automatics.

"Before we go to see if Freddy Krueger's in the yard, I think you should tell me exactly what happened."

"You're right. I'm just so shook up." She takes a deep breath. "Well, I was in the kitchen, nuking a burrito, when I heard footsteps on the deck. At first I didn't really pay any attention, but then I heard them again. Really clear."

Carver's words come back to him. "You know, it has been raining pretty hard," says Josh. "And the wind's strong. Are you sure you heard footsteps?"

She nods. "Positive. I told you, I heard shoes. And the deck creaks. The only way you could cross it without making any noise would be if you could fly." She finally lets go of him, but only to hand him the club. "Here. I'm not sure I could really bash somebody over the head."

"And I could?" He takes the club from her. Gingerly.

"What about a gun? You want one of my dad's guns?"

Naturally, the General has multiple guns. He probably has an arsenal in the basement.

"You do understand that I'm a lover, not a fighter, right?" How he wishes. In reality, of course, he is neither.

"Tilda's boyfriend does kung fu."

Then maybe she should have called him.

"I don't. I do yoga." Not quite the same thing. "I can do a warrior pose, but it's a nonviolent warrior."

"Oh." She frowns. "So you don't want to check outside? I think you're supposed to check."

Why would she think that? It's like firing a gun at your foot to see if it's loaded.

"People only do that in movies." And as soon as they step out into the pitch-black night some psycho with scythes instead of hands jumps out at them and then all you've got are blood and screaming and popcorn all over the floor. "Look, the doors and windows are all locked, right? So nobody's going to get in without our knowing. And as long as they're out there and we're in here it's all cool. My vote says you put the alarm on and we wait to see if anything else happens." And, if it does, then they call the cops.

"I suppose that makes sense." But probably not as much as he thinks. "If you're really sure . . ."

"I'm really sure." He certainly hopes he is.

They sit side by side on the sofa in the living room, looking serious and not unworried, *American Gothic* revisited—without the overalls or apron, and Josh holding the golf club instead of a pitchfork.

She's nervous as a chicken at the fox's birthday party, jumping at every noise—imagined or real. *What was that? What was that? What was that?*

He is calm and reassuring. "It's just a branch hitting the house." Or a garbage can being blown down the road. Or someone slamming a door. Or a garden shed having its roof ripped off.

He puts an arm over the back of the couch—not quite over her and not quite not—and she takes his free hand. Their phones are beside them, just in case they do need the police.

Slowly, she starts to relax.

“Maybe you were right,” she whispers as something else falls in the storm. “Maybe all I heard was the wind throwing something around. I do get kind of skittery.”

“It doesn’t matter.” He squeezes her hand. “It’s better to be safe than sorry.” Christ, now he’s sounding like his mother.

“I didn’t use to be like this,” says Jena. Nor did he. “I used to be normal. You know, I usually felt pretty safe. I didn’t really think about it. But after my mom—after her accident, I started always expecting something bad to happen. I don’t think I’ll ever be able to drive. Just the thought of it terrifies me.” She almost laughs. “But I guess everything does. That’s why I really hate to be alone.”

“Where do you hide a tree?”

She doesn’t know what he means.

“Where do you hide a tree?” repeats Josh. “In a forest. You know, because there are so many trees you’ll never find it.”

“Oh, yeah. Like that.” She almost laughs again. “Sometimes I’m afraid to even walk down the street in case something falls out of a window or a plane or something and kills me.” She leans her head against him. “But I am glad you came over, Josh. I feel safe with you.”

Safe because he has superpowers and sumo wrestlers

quake at the sight of him? Or safe because she knows he won't hit on her? She can trust him. He's one of the girls. But he doesn't want to be one of the girls. His bones are melting, his bones and his heart. *Now!* he urges himself. *Make a move now!*

Because he can't trust himself to speak, he squeezes her hand again. This time she squeezes back.

"Tilda and I are really tight and I love her and everything. She's great." Jena's voice is low and slow. "But I couldn't tell her stuff like this. Or anybody else really. They're totally normal, you know? They don't ever have weird thoughts like I do. They'd think I was nuts."

He's the one who's nuts. For God's sake, what's wrong with him? Here she is, baring her soul, and all he can think of is kissing her.

She suddenly sits up straight and looks at him. "You're not mad at me, are you?"

"Mad? Why would I be mad at you?" He'd walk through a blizzard for this moment. Maybe not barefoot, that's a little harsh, but in just his regular shoes and a light jacket.

"Why?" She must be feeling safe; she finally manages the first laugh since he arrived. "For dragging you out in the rain just to hold my hand because I'm such a baby. The General says I have to snap out of it." She lowers her voice as if the ears of the walls were all turned toward her. "Don't tell anybody, but he even sent me to a shrink."

"You're not a baby." She isn't. She's lovely. Lovely and sad and scared and lonely. "And you don't need a shrink. You're still grieving." She's an angel. An angel whose eye makeup is a little smudged, but an angel who is glad he's here.

Maybe Carver's right. Stranger things have happened.

He moves toward her. Gradually, millimeter by millimeter—pulled forward by her smile. She doesn't move away, she just keeps smiling. *Kiss her . . . kiss her . . . kiss me . . .*

He's only inches from her lips when the front door slams and the alarm goes off like a bomb.

"Jenevieve! Jenevieve! Where in God's name are you? What the hell is going on?"

Despite the fact that the sudden shock triggers freak heart palpitations, Josh automatically jumps to his feet, knocking his phone off the sofa, banging into the coffee table, and sending what was a precise stack of *Army* magazines cascading to the floor.

"Jenevieve!" The General looms in the doorway. He doesn't even glance at Josh. "Why the hell do you have all the lights on? You working for the electric company now?"

Autumn Blues

Jena kicks at the leaves scattered across her path, while beside her Tilda talks about how she's looking forward to the winter when Anton's promised to take her snowboarding. "I said, 'Isn't it a little dangerous?' " says Tilda, "and he said I didn't have to worry because he'll be with me."

Lucky Tilda.

"Sometimes I think I'm never going to get a boyfriend." If Jena were a bird her sigh would be the call of a lonesome dove. "I don't know what's wrong with me. What if I really do wind up forty and single and roommates with Josh?"

"That's not going to happen. No way." Tilda speaks with the confidence of Jehovah. "I'd never let that happen."

The confidence of Jehovah and the authority, too.

"I'm not dissing him or anything," explains Jena, feeling she may have sounded a little harsh. "Josh is a really good friend."

Even Tilda, if she knew about all the times Josh has come to Jena's aid, would have to agree with this statement. You certainly wouldn't catch Tilda unclogging the Capistranos' toilet or braving a storm to protect Jena from intruders.

"That doesn't make him boyfriend material." Tilda's laugh is light as bubbles. "I mean, Josh may be a five-star pal, but he is so totally wrong for you in so many ways that I wouldn't know where to start if you asked me to list them." She doesn't have to add that if Jena started seeing Josh he'd be the only person Jena did see—he would never fit in with the rest of Tilda's crowd.

"Oh God, no. Of course he isn't. I know that," says Jena. Not that she'd be able to explain why—especially not to herself. Jena is not a girl to overthink things. Her feelings for Josh are not so much ambiguous as unprocessed. "But who is boyfriend material? That's the multimillion-dollar question. These guys I've gone out with . . ." At least she really likes Joshua Shine. "I feel like I'm a one-woman no-guy zone."

"Don't get all angsty," says Tilda. "Help is on the way. Anton has this friend—I met him the other day after the game? He's super hot. Anyway, I think you guys would be perfect for each other."

Jena's smile is noncommittal. She's heard this before.

"This time, I know I'm right," says Tilda. "Trust me."

How dumb can you be? Dumb. Dumb. Dumb. He could win the Nobel Prize for stupidity. What a jerk. Over and over, like a video on a loop, he sees her looking at him. Waiting. And what did he do? Nothing. He really blew it this time. What's that old saying? *He who hesitates is a champion loser.* Dumb and doomed. He should have grabbed her the second she yanked him through the door. He should have said he'd been so worried about her he couldn't get to her fast enough. *Look at my shoes! Look at my clothes! I risked my life for you!* He should have told her how he feels. Failing that, when they were sitting on the couch and she leaned her head against him he shouldn't have thought about kissing her, he should have just done it. Been an action man, not an inaction ditherer.

But he didn't do the things he should have—or, possibly, shouldn't have.

And so the autumn shuffles along in a normal, autumnal way. Leaves fall, temperatures dip, days get shorter, clothes get heavier—and Josh and Jena act as if nothing almost happened.

The thing is, he doesn't know if Jena is acting or not. It could be that she's still thinking of him as roommate-not-romance material; she may have no idea how close she came to being lunged at by a boy who's like one of the girls. But Josh, of course, is acting his heart out. Is this being grown up? Hiding how you feel, pretending to be one thing when you really want to be something else? Every time he sees her he wonders what would have happened if the General hadn't charged in worrying about his electricity bill. Would Josh really have done something? Or not? He thought he was going to, but he's let himself down before. On the other hand, maybe it was better that he didn't, that the dad police arrived just in time. Or maybe it isn't. He rides up and down on the seesaw of doubt. If only she would give some sign that she did know that something almost happened: to let him know she thinks she had a close call, *whew*, or, alternatively, to indicate that she wishes the General had run out of gas two miles from home. Since she doesn't, he just wonders and frets—and pretends.

There would never be a bad time to have his dad around, but Josh figures that now would be a really good time for him still to be alive. They could have a man-to-man talk the way fathers and sons do in movies and TV shows. Not that he's aware of any of the fathers and sons he knows personally having those talks. Carver's father always tells him to ask his mother, and Sal's dad is always too busy or too tired to say anything more than "We'll talk about it later." The only man-to-man pieces of advice either of them has offered over the years are *For God's sake use a condom* (Mr. Jefferson) and *Never ride the clutch* (Mr. Salcedo). But Ethan Shine might have been different. In Josh's memories of him, he is not only always present but he's very user-friendly. Helped him with his homework. Drove him to junior chess club. Showed him how to make a perfect sundae. Josh has never been fishing in his life (he doesn't eat them, he's definitely not going to hook them and watch them die), but he has no trouble imagining him and his father sitting by a tranquil river, lines in the water, sunlight winking through the trees, talking about life. Birds would sing, bees would buzz, and Josh would tell his father all about Jena and all his doubts. In turn, Ethan would give him useful but manly advice based on experience and a realistic view of his only child (Hannah isn't realistic; she's a mother).

It's because Josh doesn't have his dad that he's been looking forward to the start of the holiday season the way someone who gets seasick on a pool float looks forward to the end of an ocean voyage. He and his mother are going to Brooklyn to spend Thanksgiving with his uncles, Walt and Mark. *What a relief it will be to be back on land!* thinks the hapless sailor. *What a relief it will be to be in a Jenevieve Capistrano–free zone for even a few days!* thinks Josh. He could use a break that doesn't involve his heart.

More than just the liberation of being away, however, is the fact that Walt is the closest Josh comes to having a male parent. Uncle Walt, his mother's brother. Blood relative. Genes in common. Man of the world. When Josh's father died, Walt stayed with them the entire summer, bonding with Josh and comforting Hannah, just his presence making things better if not actually good. Josh really likes Walt, and Walt really likes him. They text and e-mail weekly. At least once a month they talk on the phone. They have a running chess game going, each with a board set up in a corner of his bedroom. Although they see each other infrequently—visits having to be doled out between the Shines in Parsons Falls and Mark's large family that spans seaboards and continents—when they do it's always clear that the bonding worked. He can talk to Walt.

There was a time when being even a hundred miles away from home would have put Jenevieve Capistrano out of his sight if not his mind fairly firmly, but that time isn't now. This is the twenty-first century, and in the twenty-first century you are only as far away as your phone. They have barely left the driveway when Jena texts him to say that she's sorry she didn't get to say good-bye. This is a busy time of year for her. Josh and she swap texts for most of the drive. She sends him a picture of the enormous bird her father won in the turkey shoot (frozen, mercifully). Tonight she's going to the first party of the holidays at Anton's house, but Jena can't decide what to wear. What does he think? The red dress? The blue? Pictures are sent of each. Josh says she'll look terrific if she goes in overalls. Not helpful, she replies, but signs it with an *X*. He sends her pictures of their journey—funny signs, odd buildings, weird license plates, a photo of his mother shouting at the GPS when she realizes that they're lost. Jena's last text is *OMG! Gotta get ready XX.*

She sends him a selfie wearing a green dress, ready to leave for the party. He doesn't hear from her again except for a smiley face wearing a pilgrim's hat and *Don't eat 2 much XX* beside it on Thanksgiving morning.

At Walt and Mark's everyone pitches in preparing the birdless dinner. Walt and Hannah do the baking, Mark is chef and Josh is his kitchen assistant. Which keeps him busy, but not so busy that he doesn't find time to think about Jena. How was the party? How was dinner with her grandparents, cousins, aunts, and uncles? Were there fights like there usually are? Did the General undercook the turkey again? Did her family play games after dinner like his did? Was she thinking of him?

Josh and his uncle have a tradition, started at the beginning of the bonding mission after Ethan died. Whenever they visit, he and Walt spend a day together without Mark or Hannah. If they're in Parsons Falls, he and Walt take his uncles' dogs for long walks in the woods. If they're in the city, he and Walt spend a day in Manhattan (leaving Hannah and Mark to walk the dogs). Depending on the time of year, they might start at Central Park or Rockefeller Center, they might go to a museum, ride the ferry, or walk the High Line, but wherever they start, they always end in the Village, walking the same streets legendary musicians of the folk scene once walked. Walt, who teaches history, never tires of telling Josh what and who were there in the sixties and seventies, and Josh never tires of hearing it—no matter how many times he's heard it before.

They make their expedition on Black Friday when others are out being trampled in the sales. This year they go to the Tenement Museum. Walt is more interested in the stories of history's losers than of its winners. It wasn't only legendary musicians who once walked the streets of Lower Manhattan. The waves of immigrants fleeing starvation, war, and persecution in the nineteenth century all found a home here, no matter how tenuous or how difficult.

Josh's own forebears—Shines, Wolffs, Hullahans, Impys, Kesslers, and Lonnegins—were among them, starting new lives in the tenements and slums of this new city with all its promises and dreams and lies. Walt knows so much about the area that the museum staff joke they should give him a job. Afterward they roam through the Lower East Side until they finally end up in a café on Spring Street.

"So, Josh, how's life treating you these days?" asks Walt after they've sat down.

"Six of one, half dozen of the other," says Josh.

"That good?"

Josh knocks over the salt. "I have some personal stuff that's kind of driving me crazy."

Walt leans back in his chair. "I don't want to ruin the surprise or anything, but does it happen to involve a girl?"

Not only has he become irrational, he's become suspicious as well. "Who told you that?"

"I did notice you've been checking your phone a lot since you got here." Walt shakes out his napkin. "And Charley Patton mentioned something last time we talked. You know what he's like."

"Yeah. He has a big mouth like my mother."

"I think it was more concern than gossip," says Walt. "Charley says you've been a little listless lately. Not as playful as usual."

Moody. Broody. Locked in his room, playing his guitar.

"You don't have to talk about it if you don't want to."

But Josh does want to. "This is just between us, right?"

"If you don't want me to say anything to Charley Patton, I won't," Walt assures him. "It's just between us. Man to man."

They're not by a river, they're next to the window looking out on the busy city street—gray buildings and sidewalks, crammed storefronts, people hurrying past with their things to do and places to be and not even a visible spring—but, much as he fantasized about telling his father, Josh tells Walt about Jena. All the things he hasn't told anyone else. How he reacted the first time he saw her. How he climbed the tree in her front yard. How they became friends. How he can't stop thinking about her. How he almost kissed her; how he didn't.

Walt doesn't speak until he's done. "So is this the girl in the photo?"

"What photo?"

"The one your mother sent of you trying to break your back in a yoga pose."

The picture of him and Mo doing double downward dog for the class demonstration. He has no privacy; not a shred.

"Mom sent you *that*?"

"She has no secrets from me." Walt winks. "Not since I broke her code and read her diary when she was fourteen. She gave up after that."

"That's not Jena." Josh laughs.

Walt picks up his fork and puts it down again. "Oh, I thought—"

"That's Ramona Minamoto. You know her. Remember? You even gave her a ride on your motorcycle once, and she complained you drove too slow."

"*That's* Ramona? Good God!" Walt makes a well-I'll-be-damned face. "Of course I remember her. She's hard to forget. But I haven't seen her for a while. What a difference a year or two makes. She's sure grown up." He winks. The talk has deviated from what Josh envisioned, but the wink is pretty man-to-man.

"Jena's more . . ." Conservative? Conventional? "You know, more regular than Mo. She hangs out with the popular crowd."

"Ah." Walt nods. "I see. So you're worried she doesn't believe in cross-species fraternization."

That, too.

"I just think . . . you know . . . that I'm not really what she's looking for as a boyfriend."

"You never can tell with folk, you know. She may

hang out with the cool crew, but she also hangs out with you. Right?"

"Yeah." In a not-so-you'd-necessarily-notice sort of way.

"You're good friends. You said she tells you stuff she doesn't tell anybody else."

"Yeah." Rent-a-pal. There when no one else is. "And I'm the go-to guy when there's some emergency."

Walt has a thoughtful, marking-a-paper look on his face. "What kind of emergencies?"

"Oh, you know," says Josh. "Alien invasion . . . giant blood-sucking bats swarming over Parsons Falls . . . the end of civilization . . . that kind of thing."

He nods. "What happened? She locked herself out?"

"That, too."

The paper Walt is mentally marking is hovering somewhere between grades. "And you don't think that she might have a crush on you? That maybe that kind of thing is a hint?"

"I guess so. Carver thinks it might be. He says that stranger things have happened." Men have walked on the moon. Cloned sheep. Put a computer in a pair of glasses. "But I'm not exactly a babe magnet." More like a babe deterrent. Tell the girls that he's invited, and they'll all go somewhere else.

"But you know that she likes you," insists Walt. "That's what's important."

"Right. Only I don't know how I'm supposed to be able to tell how much she likes me." He looks down at his half-eaten meal and then back at his uncle. "Ramona said there'd be signs, so I made a list."

"Of course you did," says Walt. Josh is known for his lists. Mainly because he never remembers where he put them.

"There were six things on it." Starting with Jena saying she's never known anyone like him and ending with her letting him drink out of her glass, he rattles it off as if he's reading it. "But I don't know what it means," he says when he's finished. "What do you think?"

"Honestly?" asks Walt. "I think there's only one way you're going to find out for sure."

"Yeah, that's what Carver said. But what if I ruin everything? What if I say something and we're not even friends anymore?"

"Then maybe you weren't really friends to begin with." He raises his cup as if making a toast. "It'll be a new year soon, Josh. Besides, it's better to try and fail than never try."

Josh isn't sure whether that's history's winners talking or its losers.

Better to Try and Fail

Josh is resolved. He's going to tell her. He has nothing to lose. Not really. Better to be miserable in certainty than miserable in doubt. Nonetheless, he doesn't call Jena as soon as they get home on Sunday. He wants to, but he doesn't. Hang tough. Be cool. He unpacks, slowly. When he's done that, he goes over to Carver's (the long way) to pick up Charley Patton, who comes running as soon as he hears Josh's voice. At least someone missed him.

When he gets back to his house he makes himself a chamomile tea, puts on a Blind Willie McTell album, and only then does he pick up his phone.

Jena answers on the first ring. "Josh! I wasn't sure when you'd be back. It feels like you've been away for weeks." Not to him. To him it's been at least a year. "I've really missed you."

I've really missed you. Charley Patton *and* Jenevieve Capistrano. It's just as well he's sitting down.

"You did?" She has?

"Of course I did."

Hang tough. Be cool. He doesn't say, *I missed you, too.*

"Hey," says Jena, "what are you doing now? Are you busy?"

"To tell you the truth, right now I am. I'm on the phone."

She laughs. "What about getting off the phone and coming over? I really want to talk to you. I have some major stuff to tell you."

He says he has some major stuff to tell her, too.

"So you'll come over? ASAP? I really want to see you."

I want to see you. . . .

"I have some things to do first. I'll see you in an hour or two."

He's as calm as a tornado. He takes a shower—and stubs his toe on the tub. Although it's only slightly more necessary than providing a dolphin with an umbrella, he shaves—and cuts himself twice. He trims his nails—and stabs himself with the scissors. He irons his favorite shirt and his best jeans. He irons them again. He considers wearing a tie, of which he owns two—one that belonged to his dad and the guitar tie his mother gave him for his birthday—and then decides that a tie is too uncool; he's going to a romantic tryst, not a job interview. Assuming he makes it there without being hit by a car.

When Josh finally emerges from his room like a butterfly from a chrysalis, his mother is stretched out on the sofa reading a book on natural healing that Mark the nutritionist gave her.

She gives him one of her surveillance-camera looks over the top of the magazine. "Going somewhere special?"

He walks past her and into the kitchen. "No."

His back is to her, but he hears her sniff. "What's that smell?"

He pours himself a glass of water. His throat is so dry he feels as if he'd swallowed sand. "I don't smell anything." It's the cologne Walt gave him—a good-luck gift. Light but sophisticated. Masculine without laboring the point.

He doesn't have to turn around to know that she's still eyeing him. A digital surveillance camera: no film to run out.

"So where are you going?"

"I told you. Nowhere. Just going to go see the guys for a while."

"You ironed your jeans to see the guys?"

"Geez . . . Look at the time." His glass bangs against the counter. "I have to go. See you later, Mom."

The last word he hears her say is "When?" as he runs from the house, slamming the front door behind him.

As anxious as he is to see Jena, he doesn't rush, taking his time to get his heart rate down and go over what he'll say. As if the two or three hundred times he's already gone over it aren't enough. *Jena, you must know how much I like you. . . . Jena, you're the nicest and prettiest girl I've ever known. . . . Jena, I was thinking maybe we could go on a real date—you know, girl and geek, ha ha ha . . .* Maybe he shouldn't say "geek." Maybe she hasn't noticed. He doesn't want to put ideas in her head. Not that one at least. *Jena . . . Jena . . . Jena . . .* He couldn't be more nervous if he were being chased by starving lions. He walks around the block behind hers, repeating his mantra over and over: *Jena, you must know how much I like you. . . . Jena, you're the nicest and prettiest girl I've ever known. . . . Jena, I was thinking maybe we could go on a real date—you know, not as friends . . . I mean, we'd still be friends but . . . Jena . . . Jena . . . Jena . . .*

At last he stands on her corner. His palms are sweating. Should he act like it's just a regular visit, chatting about this and that and making jokes, or should he walk in, say, "Jena, there's something I have to tell you before anything else." And just blurt it out? Maybe he should have brought her flowers. Even one flower. A rose. He should have brought her a rose. A red rose. She would have been pleased, but surprised. "What's this for?" she would have asked. And then he could have told her. "The red rose means love." Does it? He thinks so. It means something. He has no idea. He takes a deep breath and marches up her front path. *We who may be about to die or at least terminally humiliate ourselves salute you.*

The door opens and his fears vanish.

"Josh!" Her face is flushed and her eyes shine. She is really happy to see him. Really, really happy. "Come on in!" She throws her arms around him. This is going to be way easier than he thought. "Oh, I am so glad you're here. I have so much to tell you!" She steps back but doesn't let go. "Oh, Josh!"

"Jena, I—"

He's never actually seen anyone jump with joy before. "Josh. Josh. Guess what! You won't believe it!"

He will. She missed him. She's so glad to see him. Of course he'll believe it.

"Josh . . ." She holds her breath for a second. "Josh—I met someone!"

Met someone . . . Met someone . . . He doesn't know what she means. *Met someone?* Someone like a movie star? Someone like the President? Met who?

"What?"

She jumps again. "You know! I met someone! I met a guy! This really cool guy!"

This can't be happening. Not now. Not to him.

"You met a guy?"

Her face is luminous as a full moon. "Yes. Can you believe it?"

He may have to.

"He's so incredible! Really incredible!" She's jumping and laughing and still holding on to him. "It's totally amazing!"

"It sure is." He wants to go home. Right this second. *Beam me up, Scotty. . . .* Go home exactly now. "That's terrific!" He can't quite manage a smile, so he puts on his chess face—give nothing away. "I can't wait to hear all about him."

He doesn't have long to wait.

His name is Simon Copeland. He's eighteen. Jena met him at the party. "I know it's only been a few days—"

Four days. Four ordinary, twenty-four-hour days.

"It must seem pretty fast—"

Faster than light.

"But I'm a hundred percent sure."

"Sure of what? That he isn't a serial killer?"

He can tell that she laughs because that's such a ridiculous idea, not because she thinks his joke is funny. *S* for Simon; *S* for serious.

"You know what I mean," says Jena. "In case it didn't work out. I don't exactly have a great track record."

Unlike Josh.

Defeat makes him daring. "You don't think it's still a little early to tell if it worked out?" asks Josh. "Maybe you should give it five days. Just to be really sure."

She laughs again: what a joker. "Oh, Josh!" No, she doesn't. It has worked out, she's absolutely certain; Jenevieve Capistrano and Simon Copeland are officially going out. What a difference a day makes. Or four.

"It's just as well the Thanksgiving break isn't longer or you'd probably be married by now."

He's never heard her titter before, but even that doesn't make him feel any better. It seems that he can forgive Jena anything.

And it isn't as if it's all doom and gloom and news so bad he wishes an asteroid would hit the earth. There is one fantastically good thing about Simon Copeland: he doesn't live in Parsons Falls, but two towns away. So at least Simon won't be in Josh's face every day. He doesn't have to fear walking down a hallway in case he sees them holding hands; in case he turns a corner and sees them enthusiastically mixing saliva.

"He's a friend of Anton's."

"Anton?"

She does have something in common with Ramona Minamoto, after all. The sigh. "Tilda's boyfriend. Remember? You see him around school all the time."

"Oh, sure. Anton." Built like a cement mixer but much better-looking.

Anton and Simon got to know each other at various countywide games, even though they're on rival teams. "Tilda said the minute she met Si she knew he and I were, like, perfect for each other. She said she could just picture us together. Isn't that too much?"

Way, way too much. The Devil must be counting the minutes until Tilda Kopel can join him in Hell.

"I wasn't even sure I should go to the party," says Jena. "I was getting my period and feeling kind of gross but Tilda made me. She said what kind of friend was I to miss Anton's party." No friend at all, obviously. "I mean, can you believe it? I almost didn't go! It makes you think, doesn't it?"

It definitely makes Josh think. She almost didn't go; she almost never met Simon. In which case, they would never have started talking; they would never have realized they were deliberately made for each other and they would never have become a couple. They would have been ships that didn't even pass in the night, not ships that crashed into each other. There would have been a different ending, one in which Josh turned up on her doorstep with a bunch of red roses and she threw herself into his arms. Not into Simon Copeland's. (Which are undoubtedly hard and muscular from all the sports he plays.) Josh has to concede that there is such a thing as Fate after all. Science and logic don't stand the chance of a single drop of water on the desert at high noon next to Fate. He pictures Fate as a miserable, troll-like creature, filled with loathing and devious schemes, cackling under its breath as it destroys another life. And Fate, it seems, really has it in for Josh.

"I don't even know what we talked about." Her laugh fizzes like a shaken bottle of soda. "I was so nervous, you know? Like I was being interviewed for an important job or something." Josh has a good idea of what that feels like. "Tilda said he's a really big deal at his school. Hyper-popular and a football hero and everything. So you can imagine how intimidating that was. I mean, *me*? Why would someone like that want to go out with *me* when he could go out with any girl he wants?" To ruin Josh's life, why else? "But Tilda was right about me and Si. She is pretty amazing like that. It's a real gift." That would be Tilda Kopel's gift, of course; not the ability to talk to horses. "Si and I really hit it off. Like, instantly. It really was like we were always supposed to meet." What Josh wonders is if Tilda has to actually boil frogs, newts, and bat wings to make a magic potion or if she can cast a spell simply by twitching her nose.

Jena is happy; really, really happy. Happy like she's six years old and it's Christmas, her birthday, and the last day of school all at once. As her friend, he should be happy, too. But he isn't, of course. In theory, maybe. In reality, losing every game of the state chess tournament wouldn't depress him this much. Even watching every one of his old vinyls melt would only come a close second.

"It's incredible," she tells him. "I never thought I'd feel like this."

Josh never thought he'd feel like this, either. Until today he believed that this thing for Jena had made him feel about as bad as he could without some major tragedy befalling his family, but that was like thinking you knew what pain is because you stubbed your toe. He should have remembered that things can always get worse. And probably will.

"Isn't that what everybody says?" asks Josh. Smiling so she thinks he's joking.

"They say that because it's true." Jena's is now the voice of experience. "You can't even imagine what it's like until it happens." She pulls her phone from her pocket. "Hey. You want to see a picture?"

"Of what?"

"Oh Josh! Stop teasing me!" She takes a playful swipe at him. "Of Simon, of course." As if there is nothing else on the planet worthy of a photograph.

This is just what was missing from his day, physical evidence. Now his misery is complete. It can't be long before the asteroid hits.

"Sure I do." Maybe he's wrong. Maybe Simon won't be handsome with a heart-shifting grin. Maybe he'll be kind of funny-looking. And short.

She taps at her phone for a few second, then holds it out to him, watching his face. Expectantly. "Well?" prompts Jena. "What do you think?"

Simon is handsome—model handsome. And tall. Very tall. Josh knows this because standing beside Simon in the photo is Jena, her head tilted against him.

"Yeah," says Josh. "He looks like a nice guy."

"He is a nice guy." Josh should probably take a picture of her now, smiling like that. In case some day he has to explain the concept of joy to an extraterrestrial. *It looks just like this.* "I can't wait for you to meet him."

A smile, of course, is no indication of happiness. People have smiled on the gallows. Josh smiles now. "Me, too."

When Simon Meets Josh

It's a cold, gray Saturday morning, outlined in frost—early enough that most people are still indoors if not in bed, and the town is still closed for business, its awnings up, its gates down, its Christmas lights dark. Josh and Ramona, bundled up in heavy jackets, scarves, hats, and gloves, are the only people on Main Street. Josh is pulling a large folding shopping cart with a bright orange liner (God forbid anyone should not notice it); Ramona carries an oversized canvas satchel over one shoulder.

"I really appreciate this," Ramona is saying as she turns into the side street next to the deli. "I couldn't do it alone."

Because of all the time she's been spending on the costumes for the school play, Ramona is late starting on her art project for the year and wants to be able to work on it over the upcoming winter break. This year's theme is "How We Live Now." Being Ramona (and her mother's daughter), she couldn't just do something straightforward like a photomontage of the town, which is what most of her class is doing. Oh no, not Ramona Minamoto. She has to re-create Main Street with found materials (found after someone else threw them out)—showing how we live and making a statement about our consumer society at the same time. Art without social or political comment is an ad, apparently. It goes without saying that Carver thinks Ramona's is a genius idea. "Nobody could ever say Ramona's just another pretty face," said Carver. But Carver isn't here lugging the cart behind him in the icy early light; he's still sound asleep, enveloped in blankets and quilts, and no doubt dreaming of solar panels and wind turbines.

"And I appreciate the enormous self-sacrifice you're making," Ramona goes on. "I do know you're not exactly a natural rag-and-bone man."

Which, if anything, is an understatement of epic proportions. Ramona was probably Dumpster diving as soon as she could walk, but Josh wasn't raised to go through other people's trash. Not only is it unhygienic, even though he knows it's better for things to be reused and recycled than to go to the landfill, it almost feels like stealing. If he'd been born in a slum, his life dependent on scavenging the city dumps, he'd probably be dead by now.

His automatic response when Ramona asked him to help her was, "No. It's really not my kind of thing." She begged him. He hesitated. She played the one-of-your-best-friends card. Which was hard to refuse. He imagined her trudging through the chilly winter morning by herself while he was at home, warm and comfortable and eating toast with Charley Patton. And remembered all the things she's done for him over the years. What kind of selfish, wishy-washy creep would refuse to give her a hand?

"Don't you think we have enough stuff now? You don't have to literally re-create the town." They've been out since dawn and have probably gathered enough of other people's garbage to make a dozen models. She has enough to make a model of all five boroughs of New York City if she wanted. "It's getting kind of late, Mo. The stores'll be opening up soon."

"Just one more stop," says Ramona, sounding as if she hasn't made that same promise three times before. "I want to check out behind Milstein's and the hardware store. That Dumpster's usually gold."

Only she would know that.

What Josh wants is to be gone before the Saturday

shoppers start arriving. He can already smell coffee and baking bagels; breakfast is about to be served. He's willing to help, but less willing to be seen. What if someone from school spots them? Someone like Mr. Burleigh. Josh already has a reputation—UFO champion, vegetarian activist, science-lab terrorist—he doesn't need to add to it with junk man.

"You worry too much," says Ramona. "If Burleigh saw us he'd probably think you're planting a bomb."

Or I don't worry enough, thinks Josh. There are already a couple of cars in the lot behind Milstein's and the hardware store.

"You know, if Sal wasn't sick, he'd've come with me—and he wouldn't be so grumpy about it." Ramona strides ahead of him.

Sal?

"Are you saying you asked Sal before you asked me?" he calls after her, but she's scrambling up into the golden Dumpster like the pro that she is and doesn't seem to hear.

Josh watches her poke through the things within reach for a few minutes, then repeats his question. "Did you ask Sal to help you before you asked me?" He's not sure why that bothers him—especially since he didn't want to come in the first place—but it does.

Ramona doesn't look around. "No. I didn't have to ask him. He offered."

"He did?" That wasn't like Sal. The only thing that would get him out of bed before noon on a Saturday would be an early breakfast meeting with one of his favorite directors. "He actually volunteered to do this?"

"Yes, Josh, he volunteered." She looks over her shoulder at him. "Which is more than you did. And he would've come, even with a fever, but his mother wouldn't let him out of the house."

"What's up with that?" It must be the play. Sal's grown obsessive about it, the way he does. That explains a lot. Besides Sal inviting Ramona to join them on movie nights. Josh often sees Sal in the Moon and Sixpence, talking to her. Which would be odd if they weren't both so involved in saying bye-bye to Birdie. Not Sal talking to Mo—that wouldn't be odd—but that he's talking to her in her mother's store is. If there is anyone more nervous around Jade Minamoto than Josh, it's Sal. Every time she sees Sal she starts yammering about "his people"—convinced that they were Mayan even though he's told her a dozen times that the Salcedos came from Spain. Why would he risk another lecture on the great, doomed city of Chichén Itzá to talk to Ramona when he doesn't have to? But the play explains it. Josh understands that. What he doesn't understand is why it irks him that Sal's around Ramona so much. She was his friend first. "I can't believe he offered to help you collect garbage today. That's not like Sal. The only thing he volunteers for is second helpings."

"Maybe he's changed." She turns around, a plastic bag filled with colored wire in her hands. She looks at him as if Sal may not be the only one who's changed.

"I guess he has." And then, even though he knows he sounds like he's about three years old, adds, "It's just that you didn't used to be so buddy-buddy."

"So? We got to know each other better from working on the play, and now we are chummy. You know, like you and Capistrano."

Somehow, from Ramona's mouth, "Capistrano" sounds like "offal" or "pig's lips."

"She has a boyfriend now, remember?" says Josh as Ramona disappears into the Dumpster. "He keeps her pretty busy."

Ramona's head appears over the rim. The hat she's wearing looks as if whoever knitted it was drunk at the time. It's a patchwork of colors decorated with loops and balls and twists. Making the whole experience of foraging behind the hardware store even more surreal. "I do remember she has a boyfriend, Josh. The Un-incredible Hulk."

"What?" How is it so much happens in the world that he knows nothing about? "You mean you met him?"

"You mean you haven't?"

"Not yet." Although sometimes he feels as if he has. Jena never stops talking about him. Simon did this . . . Simon said that . . . Simon thinks . . . Simon doesn't think . . . Simon wants to . . . As far as he can tell, Simon is everything that Josh isn't—popular, athletic, handsome, tall. And to prove that there is no end to Simon's outstanding qualities, the General loves him. Simon Copeland is the boyfriend of the General's dreams. Jena said it was like Simon was his long-lost son. (Which is not something she would ever say about Josh.) About the only things Josh doesn't know about Simon Copeland are his shoe size and the color of his toothbrush. Casually, not really very interested but consumed with curiosity, he asks, "So what's he like?"

She gives him a look—the look of someone who is already tired of the conversation. "I didn't really get to know him in a deep and intimate way, Josh. He came to pick Capistrano up from a meeting and she introduced him to the group. You know, 'Hey, everybody, this is Simon.' It didn't give us a real chance to bond."

She ducks below the top of the Dumpster again.

"But you think he's un-incredible."

Her voice rises above the filthy, green bin. "I'm pretty sure that's a minority opinion. Especially if you're him. But, like I said, I didn't have a chance to give him an in-depth psychological assessment. Anyway, I only said he was the Un-incredible Hulk because he's big but he isn't green. Rumor has it that he's an awesome football player."

Conscious that if anyone does come into the parking lot they're going to think he's talking to a Dumpster, Josh says, "That's what I heard."

"Then it must be true. Anyway, I guess he's okay," says Ramona's disembodied voice with all the enthusiasm of someone choosing a pair of white socks. "If you like that kind of thing." She pops up again. "I need your help. See if you can find something to stand on."

He drags a garbage can over to the side of the Dumpster and climbs on top. If it were any less stable he'd be on the ground. He takes hold of the edge of the container and peers over. She has a large box in her hands; there are two more beside her.

"Tiles!" she shouts as someone else might shout *Gold!* "Linoleum tiles! Isn't this fantabulous? And they're all different colors and patterns. I can make the buildings and streets mosaics. It'll be incredible."

“I thought you were making a model of Parsons Falls, not Philly or Barcelona.”

“It’s an art project. Remember? In art you’re supposed to use your imagination.”

He is using his imagination. He’s imagining himself heaving the tiles out of the Dumpster and breaking his neck. “Aren’t those boxes kind of heavy?”

“Yes, Joshua, they are kind of heavy.” The loops and twists and balls on her hat all bounce with vexation. “That’s why I need your help. I’ll hand it up to you. You grab the end and balance it on the rim. Then I’ll climb over and you can pass it down to me. We should be able to manage it together.”

Josh looks at the box. Warily. Balefully. What if it’s even heavier than it looks? What if it slips out of his control?

“What if you do it sometime this morning?” prompts Ramona.

He grabs the end. The box is even heavier than it looks. And treacherously unwieldy. To add to his difficulties, gravity is against him. As is the garbage can beneath his feet. Although this is something he’s never actually done, he feels as if he’s trying to guide the Eiffel Tower over a wall while standing in a rowboat on a choppy sea.

"It might be faster if you used two hands," suggests Ramona.

It might also be the end of his precious young life.

"It'd be even faster if I used four," snaps Josh.

He is concentrating so hard on trying to steady the box and not topple over that it isn't until he hears his name being called from somewhere other than the Dumpster that he realizes someone else has come into the parking lot.

"Josh? Josh, is that you?"

He knows that voice. Of all the parking lots in all the world, she has to come to this one. Now. Not a half hour from now, not tomorrow. Right at this very moment in time. Shutdown. He stops breathing; every cell in his body locks. What could he possibly have done to make Fate hate him so much?

"What are you doing?" shouts Ramona from inside the bin. "Why did you stop? I can't hold it like this." Gravity is against her as well.

Instead of answering Ramona, he looks behind him.

"Oh my God, Josh! It is you!"

And, as if twisted Fate has outdone itself to bring them together at this time and in this place, it is, of course, Jenevieve Capistrano standing behind him. This time he's pretty sure that she's laughing at him, not with him. Next to Jenevieve Capistrano, holding her hand, is Simon Copeland. Of course. Who else would it be? Simon is definitely laughing at him.

"Josh!" There is an unusual note of panic in Ramona's voice, but Josh doesn't hear it. "Josh! I can't hold it!" But all Josh hears is Jena asking him what he's doing hauling garbage out of the container.

The next thing he hears is the box hitting the ground. To prove that even when everything's going wrong, miracles can happen, he manages not to fall on top of it.

It is Simon who helps him up.

"Wow, I never thought we'd run into you like this," laughs Jena. "Talk about weird!"

Does she mean him, or just that they're in the lot behind the hardware store on a Saturday morning?

"So you're Josh," says Simon. "I didn't expect to see you climbing into a Dumpster. I thought your speciality was trees." He is not only outrageously good-looking; he has an easy confidence that is almost palpable—and that makes him doubly attractive. Even Josh can see that. Much as he'd prefer not to. "I've heard a lot about you."

Polite. Friendly. Even to someone who just fell off a garbage can.

"Really? I haven't heard anything about you."

Simon looks as if something cold just slapped him in

the face, but Jena laughs. "He's joking," she says. "Didn't I say he's really funny?"

"Oh, he's hysterical!" Suddenly Ramona vaults out of the Dumpster, landing neatly on the ground beside them. The poster girl for the benefits of yoga. "I haven't stopped laughing all morning. It may kill me." She gives Josh a look as pointed as a needle. "Especially when he let the box go."

Josh isn't sure whether the stunned silence following Ramona's arrival is because it is so sudden and dramatic, or because, as tall as Simon, she seems to tower over all three of them in her bizarre hat, wearing a too-large man's tweed overcoat, striped leggings, and motorcycle boots. He isn't sure what she looks like, but there's a good possibility that it's nothing from the planet Earth. Even Josh, with his ponytail and wearing his gathering-garbage clothes (his oldest jeans, the sneakers Charley Patton uses as scratching mats, and a jacket that was in the way of a toppled can of red paint) looks normal in comparison; Jena and Simon look positively dressed up.

Jena breaks the silence "You two met the other day?" she says, making it a question. "At the drama club meeting? Ramona Minamoto. Simon Copeland. Ramona's our costume designer."

Simon, who hasn't taken his eyes off Ramona since

she catapulted into their midst, says, "Costume designer." He nods, considering the implications of this information. "Is that why you were in the Dumpster?"

"No. My trusty companion and I were looking for stuff for my art project. What about you two? Hot date in the parking lot before the stores open?"

Once again, only Jena laughs. "We're meeting some of Si's friends for breakfast."

Simon had let go of Jena to help up Josh, but now he takes her hand again. "And we better get a move on, baby. You know I don't like to be late."

As they walk away, Ramona says, "Speak of the linebacker and he shall appear." She looks over at Josh. "So now you met him."

"Yeah, now I met him." And Simon met Josh. "He seems okay."

"No, he doesn't. I've changed my mind." She makes a that-doesn't-taste-right face. "*Baby!* I hate guys who call girls 'baby.' It's diminishing. It's better than 'ho,' but not a lot."

Josh isn't listening. He watches Simon and his baby—talking and butting against each other like playful horses—disappear out of sight. *Be glad for her,* he admonishes himself. *Look how happy she is!* But all he can think is: *it should have been me.*

Hope Is Ill

People live on the frozen tundra. People survive penal colonies, years of solitary imprisonment and concentration camps. People live through wars, disease, famine, and personal tragedies that could make the mountains cry. When you think about it like that, what's Simon Copeland compared to the Black Death, slavery, the Trail of Tears, concentration camps, or Stalin's gulag camps? Not even a minor irritation, really. He's just a good-looking boy who can tackle. Some day he'll be a lot less good-looking and he'll be lucky if he can walk, never mind tackle, because of old football injuries. Who'll be laughing then? With these thoughts firm in his mind, Josh gets used to the idea that Jena has a boyfriend. More or less.

Hope is an odd thing. Looked at logically, hope is no more than a wish that things turn out well or get better.

Whatever we do—get in cars, climb mountains, walk down the street, eat junk food, paddle across the Atlantic in a kayak, play roulette—we do because we trust that everything will be all right; we hope so. That the car won't crash, that we won't fall off the mountain, that we won't be struck by lightning, that we won't destroy our body, that we won't be lost at sea—that we'll win. If we knew for certain that we'd die in an auto accident, disappear into an abyss, have a heart attack in the parking lot where we stopped for ice cream, drown, or lose every cent we had, we wouldn't do any of those things. Indeed, if we didn't live in hope more than in reality, few of us would bother getting up in the morning. *What's the point? We're all doomed.*

Josh may have accepted the fact of Simon, but he was still holding on to the hope that he could sit Simon out. Okay, he told himself, Simon made it through the first-date test, and on into the second and third dates and official boyfriend status, but how long could it be before some fatal flaw surfaced? Eventually, Simon would blow over like a storm cloud, and the sun would shine on Josh once more. But then he met Simon, and Hope became ill and began to fade fast. Even Josh can see that Simon is pretty terrific (if you like that kind of thing). Pleasant.

Friendly. Personable. Simon likes who he is, so everybody else likes him, too. If he knows insecurity it's as something that happens to others. Simon is the teenager adults love—popular, talented, a natural at everything. The kid they want their children to be. No problems here. No dark depths or unpleasant surprises. No doubts about his future, either. They can imagine the man he'll grow into and they like him, too. Simon is the anti-weird, the boy you can rely on to do what you think he should. No wonder the General loves him. No wonder Jena thinks the center of our solar system has shifted from the sun to the star linebacker of Smittstown High. Every new thing Josh hears about Simon adds a new symptom to Hope's malady. Headache. Fever. Difficulty breathing. Arrhythmia. Dizzy spells. Nausea.

Mercifully, Simon could only be busier if he never slept. Besides school and all his extracurricular activities, he coaches an elementary school team and works part-time for his father's landscaping firm. Jena usually sees him only on weekends. "Thank God we live in the twenty-first century," says Jena. "At least we can pretty much be together even if we're apart." They spend hours together every night—he in his house and she in hers. You have to hope they have good cell phone plans. "I mean, really, can you imagine if we didn't have Snapchat? I'd probably forget what he looks like!"

What a shame that would be.

Josh is philosophical about his own lack of opportunities to see Simon again. As far as Josh is concerned, meeting Simon is one of those things, like nearly drowning, that you only have to do once to know you don't really want to do it again. But Fate, of course, has other ideas. Josh has done his best to forget what Simon looks like and almost succeeded when—like a gift from a bad fairy determined to ruin your holidays—he sees him again.

It's only days before Christmas. Every weekend in December, Josh has been busking by the war memorial at the foot of town, where the buses to the mall stop. Ramona, working in the gallery, makes him eat his lunch in the office with her and brings him cups of herbal tea through the day so he doesn't perish from the cold. Sometimes Sal, who has a seasonal job at the gourmet deli, joins them.

One Saturday Ramona turned up in a red cape with a silver ribbon wound through her hair and her violin under her arm. "People want to hear carols and 'Rudolph the Red-Nosed Reindeer,'" said Ramona. "Not 'Columbus Stockade Blues.'" He made more money in an hour than he was making in a day, and the crowd that had gathered sang along to "O Holy Night." "I figured if I didn't help out you'd never get enough to buy all your presents," said Ramona. Among other things, a necklace for his mother, a new scratch pad for Charley Patton, a cookbook for his uncles, and a silver tree charm for Jena. He didn't mention the charm. "You don't think maybe you're stereotyping?" asked Ramona. Because he was getting Charley a scratch pad? "No, dope. Because you're getting your uncles a cookbook." Josh pointed out that they like to cook.

On this Saturday, however, Josh is alone — and oddly missing Ramona. Ramona is not only fun to play with but attracts a crowd — possibly because she plays so well, or possibly because of the red cape, or possibly because, with him beside her, it looks as if she's brought an elf with her for the occasion. He's playing a spirited version of "Here Comes Santa Claus" when someone throws five dollars into his case. He looks over to see Jenevieve Capistrano smiling at him. Beside her is Simon Copeland; Simon Copeland isn't smiling. When Josh finishes the song Jena claps so much that even people just passing by join in. Though not Simon, who stands straight and tight — as if he's desperate to get to the bathroom.

"That was great," says Jena. "You're really good." Which seems to come as a surprise. "I didn't know you played stuff like that. I thought you only did old songs."

"That is an old song. You missed 'God Rest Ye Merry, Gentlemen.' That's even older."

She laughs. "You know what I mean. Folk music."

"Blues mainly," says Josh. "But I try not to be inflexible."

She puts a hand on Simon's arm. "You remember Simon."

"How could I forget?"

"And I remember Josh," says Simon. Making it clear why he remembers him—because he was Dumpster diving and fell off a garbage can—without actually saying so. He nods at the open guitar case. "I'm surprised they let you busk down here. Isn't there a town ordinance?" Making it clear that he thinks busking is one very small step away from begging and not necessarily in the right direction—but without actually saying that either.

"It's Christmas," says Josh. "Peace and goodwill to all men, right?" Though, on second thought, perhaps not every last man.

Simon smiles. "Right."

"We're on our way to the Moon and Sixpence," says Jena. "Simon's looking for something for his mom."

Simon nods. "My mom loves Americana."

"Well, that's the place to go," says Josh. "If Betsy Ross were alive she'd be selling her flags there."

"Tilda's having her party tonight," offers Jena. "I figure I can get her a little something there, too. Maybe earrings."

"Good idea," says Josh. "I did notice she definitely has ears."

He will probably never make Simon laugh.

They stand there smiling at each other for a few seconds, awkward as cats on stilts. Around them the town bustles—talk and laughter, traffic and hurrying feet—but they've become the Bermuda Triangle of Parsons Falls, still smiling but silent.

Simon adjusts his arm around Jena. "You play something, don't you? I mean besides the guitar. What is it again?"

"The mandolin," says Josh. "Mandolin and guitar. And a little harmonica."

Simon's smile does nothing to warm the afternoon. He shakes his head. "No, I meant, what game?"

"Chess."

"Oh, right," says Simon. And finally laughs. "I knew it couldn't be basketball."

Hope Dies

Jena and Simon aren't the only ones with a festive gathering to go to tonight. Which is a good thing. If he had nothing particular to do, Josh would undoubtedly spend the night imagining Jena and Simon making out in some dim corner of the party. In its dark, airless, and lonely room, Hope develops a bad cough. But, because Sal and Carver will be out of town until New Year's, Sal has invited everyone to his house for a pre-Christmas hang-out (the Pod Squad plus two, as Josh thinks of them now that Ramona and Zara have become part of the group). "Pretzels shaped like Christmas trees and cookies shaped like stars," promised Sal. "Plus the black-and-white version of *It's a Wonderful Life*." Eat your heart out, Tilda Kopel.

By the time he gets home, his mother has already gone out for the evening. Josh makes himself some supper, and he and Charley Patton share it while they listen to Bob Dylan's Christmas album. When they're done eating, Josh takes a shower and starts to get ready to go out himself.

Josh is drying his hair when the doorbell rings. Charley Patton sits up, eyes wide and ears pointing due north, in watch-cat mode. Carver said he'd walk over to Sal's with him. Josh checks the time; Carver's early. He must really like pretzels shaped like Christmas trees. The bell rings again. Urgently. "Hold on, I'm coming," he calls as he drops the towel and lopes to the door.

At first he thinks it must be raining because her face is so wet.

"Jena!" He peers behind her, but the night is cold and clear. "What's wrong? What are you doing here?" He gives another peer into the night. "Where's Simon?"

"Oh, Josh!" Sobbing, she flings herself into his arms. "I'm sorry. You're probably busy, but I didn't know what else to do."

"Are you all right? What the hell happened?" Holding her, he moves backward, pulling her into the house with him. It's almost as if they're dancing—something he's tried to imagine, except, of course, that she's never in tears. He steers her toward the sofa. "Come over here and sit down."

Several worst-case scenarios gallop through his mind in the seconds between her throwing herself at him and him getting her into the living room.

"I'm okay." She drops onto the couch, wiping at the tears with the back of her hand, smudging a band of black across her eyes so that she looks like a raccoon. A very pretty raccoon wearing dangling earrings and a sparkly dress, but a raccoon nonetheless. "I just—" Fresh tears start to fall.

He hovers over her heaving shoulders. He doesn't see any blood or bruises; her clothes aren't torn. Those have to be good signs. "Tell me what happened. Is it Simon?" The thug. The malevolent creep. "What did he do? Are you sure you're okay?" If Simon hurt her, Josh will have to get Ramona to beat him up.

"I-It-it was just so horri—" She chokes and snuffles and sobs. Most people look fairly grotesque when they weep uncontrollably, but not Jena. He has the urge to hug her, snot and all.

"Take it easy, Jen." Josh perches on the arm of the sofa, uselessly patting her shoulder. "There's no rush." They have all night.

It doesn't take quite that long, but it does take a while for her to calm down enough to force the terrible words out of her mouth.

"We — we had a fight. A — a — a really big fight."

"A fight?" Chrissake, is that all? "A word fight, right? Nobody threw any punches?"

"Of course a word fight," says Jena. "Simon would never hit me."

Their first fight. Hope looks up, considering the possibility of finally getting off its sickbed.

But, technically, it wasn't their first fight. The first fight was last week. They were going to the movies. Simon wanted to see an action movie, all special effects and graphic violence. Jena wanted to see a romantic comedy everybody was talking about. Everybody who wasn't male. She thought it would be a nice date movie. But Simon wasn't in the mood for a sappy chick flick; he'd be asleep before the opening credits were done. Jena gave in. The important thing was to be together. So they went to Simon's movie; she was bored and he fell asleep. The technical fight happened after he woke up, when Jena pointed out that since she was the one who stayed awake, they should have gone to something she wanted to see. Simon said it wouldn't kill her to be a little understanding; Jena said it wouldn't kill him, either. They didn't speak for ten minutes.

"But this was way different, Josh. This was super awful. . . ." While she's trying to control the sobs, he dashes into the bathroom and comes back with a box of tissues. "Guggleblug," she mumbles, and blows her nose. When she's more composed, she says, "I never knew what a jerk he can be."

You should've asked me.

"And so mean. You wouldn't believe how mean he was. Really gross and mean."

Prince Charming with fangs. Hope is feeling so much better it's sitting up and managing a smile.

"I couldn't believe it. He was really, really horrible," she burbles. "It was like if you were sitting next to Charley Patton and he suddenly turned into a man-eating tiger. Think how you'd feel!"

If Charley turned into a man-eating tiger Josh wouldn't feel anything for very long.

She smiles. Feebly.

"Why don't I fix you a soothing tea? Help you relax."

"I don't want to relax. I'm too angry to relax." As living proof of this statement, she stands up and starts to pace. "I'm never going to speak to that creep again."

"You're upset now. I'm sure—"

"So am I sure," fumes Jena. "Just wait'll you hear what he did."

Josh moves to the sofa proper, more ears than a field of corn. He can hardly wait.

Simon came to pick her up for the party, but she wasn't ready. "I know he's very punctual and everything, but I mean, give me a break. It's the first really special party I've been to since we came here. Much bigger than the one at Thanksgiving. I couldn't just put on any old thing and brush my hair, could I?" Absolutely not. "I had a lot to do. I said that. Didn't you hear me say that? That I needed time?" Josh thinks that time was definitely mentioned. "And it wasn't my fault we were out all afternoon shopping. Si was the one who took hours picking a present for his mom. I got earrings for Tilda in, like, a minute and a half, but he had to look at practically everything in the store. He's super, super fussy. Just like the General." Which would be another thing she hadn't known about Simon. "So big deal, he had to talk to my dad for a little while. It's not like a new kind of torture. They like each other." Josh doesn't ask how little the while was. He knows what it's like to wait for Jena. If you want her to go somewhere at six, you tell her you have to leave at five. "So he was all normal and sweet until we got in the car, and then he freaked out."

The selfish swine.

"You should've heard him, Josh. How I ruined everything. How I'm so self-absorbed. How I never think about him. He said people have made dresses in less time than it takes me to put one on!"

What a moment to find something Simon Copeland said funny! Hope, already on its feet, gives Josh a hug.

"I know a relationship's about give and take and compromise and all that stuff," Jena steams on, in danger of wearing a path in the carpet, "but I really thought he was being ridiculous. I mean, really? Because I was a little late he acts like I destroyed the civilized world? Don't you think he was being ridiculous? Tell me honestly. Don't try to spare my feelings."

"He sounds way over the top to me." Totally ludicrous. He might as well have been dressed like a clown and shaking a tambourine.

"And then he got all snotty and said he'd been running around like crazy for weeks and had this insane practice yesterday and was totally exhausted and when he got home after we went shopping he had to help his dad replace some bulbs that burned out in their roof display and have supper and everything and he still managed to be on time so why couldn't I?"

Josh's expression is sympathetic—but inside he's cheering, and Hope is cheering, too. The fatal flaw has finally appeared.

"And you know what else he said? He said I should try to empathize more with other people!" Her rage has finally stopped the tears, but her eyes still shine. "Me! I was the one who wasn't being empathetic. How unfair is that?"

Now is probably not the moment to point out that when two people are having an argument they both think they're right.

"Then the shit really hit the fan. I mean, like, seriously. It was super insane. I don't think I've ever yelled at anyone like that before. And no one's ever yelled at me like that, either. Not even the General, and yelling was part of his job." She suddenly sits down again, leaning her head against him.

He puts a hand on her shoulder. "I bet Simon's really sorry. He was tired. And Christmas is very stressful. I'm sure he knows he was wrong."

"You bet he was wrong." He's never before heard her make a sound he associates with horses. "And if he's not sorry now, he will be. Because we are through with a capital *T*."

"I'm sure once you both have a chance to—"

"No. It's over." The tiny Christmas balls hanging from her ears swing madly as she shakes her head. "I told him he was the one who'd ruined everything. I was really looking forward to this party, and now I'd rather be stuck in an elevator full of people with bad breath. I told him to pull over and let me out of the car. I said I wouldn't go to heaven with him if Saint Peter himself was waving us through the gates."

It has to be asked. "What did he say to that?"

"He said I didn't have to worry. He had no intention of driving me anywhere, and he pulled over and let me out of the car." She yanked another tissue from the box and wiped at her eyes. "So I came to you."

Calmer now, she peers at him as if she couldn't see him before. "Is your hair wet?"

"Just a little damp."

"You're not wearing a shirt."

Maybe Simon was just a little right about self-absorbed.

"I just got out of the shower."

"Oh God!" She claps a hand to her mouth. "I didn't mean to interrupt anything. If you're busy—"

"I'm not busy. I was dirty, that's all. Why don't you let me make you that tea?"

She does remember how to smile. "Is it flowers?"

"Yeah. It's flowers. But I guarantee it'll make you feel better."

"Okay. If you guarantee it."

He can't believe his luck. She had a fight with Dream Boy. She came to Josh for comfort and support. She threw herself in his arms (though it was, of course, more like he was in her arms). She's not going to be making out with Simon in some darkened corner of the Kopel house; she's going to be drinking flower tea with Josh. He will never ever complain about Fate again. Merry Christmas, Joshua Shine! Hope is ringing bells.

He puts on the kettle, then races into the bedroom. He calls Carver to tell him he's not going tonight after all. Carver wants to know why not. "Not feeling so hot," says Josh. "Probably because I was standing in the cold half the day singing 'Frosty the Snowman.'" Then he calls Sal. "But I won't see you till the new year," says Sal. "It's not like you have to do anything except sit. You really feel that crappy?" Josh says, yes, really. "Did you tell Ramona?" asks Sal. And why would he do that? "She'll notice I'm not there and figure it out for herself," says Josh. He left the shirt he planned to wear on his bed. Charley Patton, thinking it was laid there for him, is asleep on it. Josh tries brushing off the cat hairs, then rummages on his desk for tape, but that doesn't work very well, either. By the time he gets back to the kitchen it looks as if a steam locomotive has just passed through. He somehow burns himself grabbing for the handle. He makes the tea. Then he decides that crying may have made Jena hungry. He opens a box of cookies, puts some on a plate, and puts that and the cups on a tray. Sugar. She might want sugar. He puts the sugar, a spoon, and a saucer for the teabags on the tray, too. Perfect! The host with the most.

As Josh comes into the living room, he notices that something has changed. He can feel Hope having a relapse. Jena is no longer slumped on the sofa, eye shadow and eyeliner smeared around her eyes. Her makeup's been repaired, and she's standing up and putting on her jacket. She's smiling. A lot. So much that someone just arriving would never guess that she'd been sobbing her heart out only minutes ago.

"Simon just called." Her voice is as bright and happy as her smile. Apparently Simon is no longer a creep. It truly is the season for miracles. "He's coming to get me."

Josh holds out the tray. "What about the tea?"

"Oh, Josh, I'm really sorry. You've been so great. But you were totally right. Si's really sorry. You should have heard him apologizing. And, well, you know . . ."

A horn sounds in front of the house.

He knows now.

Josh watches her run down the front path and get into Simon's car. He sees them kiss. He feels as if he's jumped out of a plane and his parachute failed to open.

And then he hears Hope die.

Unhappy New Year

Christmas came. Josh and his mother went to the Minamotos' for dinner—tamales, declared by Jade Minamoto to be a holiday tradition, just not one that originated north of the border—and a game of charades that left them all exhausted with laughter. Ramona was ecstatic over the yoga DVD Josh gave her; her gift to him was a picture of them doing double bridge together, in a frame she made herself from the linoleum tiles they'd eventually rescued from the dumpster. Jena texted him in the evening to thank him for the silver tree charm, *XX*, but she was busy with Simon and he didn't see her again until school started.

And so Christmas went.

And so came another year.

"What a happy freaking New Year this is turning out to be!" Jena drops onto the sofa like a stone. A large and very angry stone. A stone that's been chipping the polish off its nails. "Really, Josh. I mean, it's only just started and already it's major bad news. I can't wait for February. February's usually depressing enough, all dark and miserable, but this year it's bound to top itself. Do something really awesome."

"You mean like a vampire invasion of Parsons Falls?" Besides unblocking the Capistrano toilet and protecting Jena from intruders, it has become his job to make her laugh. "Can you picture Mr. Burleigh wearing a necklace of garlic and a crucifix?"

She manages a smile, bleak as February. "They'd probably kill us all."

"Not necessarily," says Josh. "You might not die. You might become a creature of the night and live forever."

"Stop trying to cheer me up." Jena grabs a cushion and hugs it against her. "This is serious. If I was smart I'd dump Simon right now. That's what I'd do if I had any brains."

If she was smart, she'd have dumped Simon the day she met him.

"I know that's what I should do. Just end it. Before he makes me totally nuts."

So why don't you? Cut the cord. Push the button. Slam the door in his handsome face.

Josh puts their drinks and a bowl of chips on the coffee table. "Don't tell me — let me guess. You and Simon had another fight." Never mind the vampires, next thing you know, there will be cows flying over Parsons Falls and rabbits falling on the rooftops instead of snow.

Jena hugs the cushion harder. "Ha. Ha. Ha."

And that is how the new year has been going. Jena and Simon fight, then Jena and Simon make up; they make up; they fight. One minute Jena and Simon are the twenty-first-century Romeo and Juliet (but without the family feud, poetic language, and shadow of doom hanging over them), and the next minute they've had another blowup, and are more like Captain Kirk and Khan. Sometimes after an argument they aren't speaking for minutes, and other times for hours. The record so far is a day and a half.

When she isn't volcanically mad at him, Jena says that the reason she and Si argue so much is because they're such passionate people. "It's a very highly charged relationship," explained Jena.

Like an electric chair, thought Josh.

They can argue about anything and everything — from what kind of topping to get on their pizza to the long-term effects of slamming a car door too hard. There is nothing so insignificant that the two of them can't make it into a case worthy of being heard at an international court of law.

"Isn't it pretty exhausting?" asked Josh. It definitely exhausts him.

Jena said, "Not really, I mean, it kind of makes you feel alive."

"A good version of 'Mary, Don't You Weep' does that, too," said Josh,

Nonetheless, if you happen to be Josh, the best thing about this—apart from the fact that the Capistrano-Copeland relationship seems about as stable as a rabbit on skates riding on the back of a tortoise—is that he is now the go-to guy for couples counseling as well as emergencies. Since they are always fighting, Josh now sees Jena as much as Simon does.

"So what was it this time?" asks Josh. "You tie your laces the wrong way?"

"It's not funny." She definitely doesn't look as if she thinks it's funny. She looks as if she's never laughed in her life. "You think I'm crazy putting up with him, don't you? You think I should dump him."

Right in the middle of the ocean. Weighted down with a couple of buildings and a tank or two. Any ocean will do.

"I never said that," says Josh. Though God knows there have been enough opportunities to make the suggestion.

Their relationship is like a war that is occasionally interrupted by periods of peace. "So, seriously, what's it about this time?" He sits down beside her.

She smiles sourly. "Not shoelaces." She tosses the cushion onto the couch. "Some stupid football game, what else?" Making football sound like something disgusting and possibly depraved. "He broke our date so he can watch some stupid game with his buddies."

Simon's an idiot. He should have lied. Even football heroes must get sick once in a while. It's not like he didn't know how she'd react.

"But that's what guys do. Not break dates. Watch football together." This, as we know, is hearsay, of course. But though Josh's own experience of watching football games is nonexistent, he does understand that it's not something you do alone. It's a herd activity. Like cows watching someone cross a field. "Maybe it's a special game or something." Although he did think the special games had passed, since Simon spent New Year's Day watching the Rose Bowl. (Josh spent it consoling Jena.) "And you know how Simon is about football. Expecting him to miss a special game is like expecting the Pope to miss Christmas."

"And what am I? Pot noodles?" If Jena were a cartoon and not a human being there would be smoke pouring out of her ears. "I said I'd watch it with him. Which I think was pretty nice of me. But oh no, he always watches with the guys. It's their *ritual*." Not a ritual like dyeing eggs for Easter, obviously; more like sacrificing newborn goats at a full moon. "God forbid he should change his *ritual* just to spend a Saturday night with *me*. The world would probably end."

Josh wouldn't break a date with Jena if he had acute appendicitis. He'd rather die in her arms.

"Jocks," Josh jokes. "Who can understand them?"

"Who wants to?" If Josh isn't careful she's going to be mad at him, too. "So what do you think?" A lot of people look like deformed potatoes when they scowl, but Jena still looks pretty. Just unhappy. "You do think I should dump him, don't you?"

"It's up to you, Jen. It's your life. I'm not going to tell you what to do." *No matter how much I'd like to.*

"But you must think I'm nuts, right? Putting up with him and all his crap. Everybody must think I am. Label me 'loser' or what?"

She couldn't be more nuts without turning into a bag of almonds. But rather than lie or tell the truth, he sidesteps the question. "I don't think everybody thinks you're nuts. I bet you're the only person he annoys so much. Everybody else likes him. Remember you told me how popular he is? School legend and everything?" To be fair, though, even Josh would probably like Simon if it weren't for Jena. Not a lot. Not enough to want to be stranded on an iceberg with him or give him a kidney—but enough not to really want him stuck in the middle of the Atlantic trying to drink seawater and to fish with his hands, either. "They'd probably question your sanity if you broke up with him."

"That's what Tilda says," says Jena. Of course it is. Tilda likes Simon, the government seal of approval. "She says I'd be out of my mind to break up with him. She says the girls are lined up around the block to take my place. It'd be like dumping Prince Charming." Jena groans. "But what if I go out of my mind if I don't break up with him? I dig the passion and everything, but I don't know if I can take the stress."

"You don't have to listen to anybody else," says Josh. "Not Tilda. Not me. Not all the girls who are sitting on the sidewalk in front of Simon's house waiting for you to tell him it's over. What you do is nobody's business but your own. You have to do what you think's right."

"That's easy for you to say," says Jena.

Because he looks like a small nocturnal primate and will never find himself in this sort of predicament? Because everybody thinks he's crazy already? Because he has "loser" stamped all over him in glow-in-the-dark ink? He can't bring himself to ask for clarification.

She gives it anyway. "Because you're not like me, Josh. You don't care what people think. You always do what you think's right. You don't just go along with what everybody else is doing so they like you. You don't care if you're popular or if people think you're a little weird."

Does she think he goes out of his way to be odd, to be different? That when he was in elementary school he decided it was better to be bullied, made fun of and excluded from all the other reindeer games than to go along with everybody else? *Let's take that road with all the rubble and pitfalls in it, build some character!*

"I didn't choose to be short and funny-looking, Jena, and I didn't choose how I am. It's just me. I've always been like this."

Her mouth shrugs, her shoulders shrug, her foot bangs against the coffee table. "But that's just it, isn't it? I've never been like that. I know you probably think I'm pretty shallow—okay, *very* shallow—and sometimes part of me wishes I could be more like you. But I can't. I can't help it. This is me. I really care what other people think about me. I don't always want to follow the leader, but it's so much easier. I want to be liked."

"Everybody wants to be liked." Does she think, given

the choice, anyone would go for being disliked? "I know I do."

"No, you don't. Not the way I do. Fitting in is really important to me." Her hands beat the air like lost birds. "You don't care about being . . ."

Ridiculed? Pitied? Ignored? Disliked by the General? Looked down on by Simon? The boy who, years from now, when people flip through their yearbooks, will be the boy they don't remember at all? *Who the hell is that?*

"In the popular group."

He strikes a bravura pose. "I'm pretty popular in my group." And her friends aren't. Nobody cares about them except themselves.

"It's not the same. I mean popular like a celebrity. Like Simon. At his school, he's like a celebrity. People admire him. They wish they could be him."

Josh can definitely get that. He wishes he could be Simon. Not the football hero, big-man-on-campus part—just the part where he kisses Jena.

"So is that why you can't tell him to make a new try, Si? Because he's as popular as money?"

She doesn't answer that. Instead, she puts her hand to her mouth as if she just remembered that she left the front door open and the penguins are escaping. Her eyes widen, making them look even bluer. "OhmyGod, Josh.

I just realized. I didn't ask if you changed your plans so you could hold my hand and listen to me moan."

"It wasn't anything important." The band can practice without him. They're playing Lucille Furimsky's birthday party at the end of the month, not some big arena. He picks up the remote. "I'd rather watch a movie with you."

Jena leans against him the way a cat would—scattering peanuts on him and the sofa the way a cat wouldn't. "Simon always lets me down, but not you. You're always there for me."

Both these statements are true. Something's always coming up at the last minute for Simon. Or, memory like a busted sieve, he forgets he's seeing Jena and makes other plans. Or he strains something playing football or scaling a mountain or jumping between buildings. Or they have a fight. And Josh steps in. Good old Josh, faithful and loyal. He was probably a dog in a previous life.

She squeezes his arm. "What would I do if you weren't my friend?"

Josh presses the power button. "I guess you'd have to marry me."

Jena laughs.

Life Goes On

Sal comes to an abrupt stop outside the Moon and Sixpence. Ramona is in the window, filling it with hearts. Heart cushions. Heart wind chimes. Quilts, scarves, aprons, and sweaters, all covered with hearts. Hearts made of willow branches, made of hangers, and made of used CDs—all of them floating on red ribbons attached to the ceiling. Sal's own heart does what it always does when he sees Ramona unexpectedly: it misses a beat. And, although he has somewhere else to be and is already running late, he has a sudden brainwave and goes inside, accompanied by the gentle *click-clack* of the bamboo chimes and a big smile.

"Oh, God, busted being the Hallmark handmaiden," laughs Ramona as Sal steps through the door. She takes a heart-shaped wooden tray from the red stool beside her and holds it up like a shield. "Don't blame me. My mother made me do it. You know I'm not the sentimental type."

"Me neither," says Sal. Which isn't strictly true. "But seeing you decorating the window for the big love-in gave me this fantastic idea."

"Really? A fantastic idea about Valentine's?" She looks as if she doesn't believe him. "And what's that?"

Sal grins. "We have the alternative Valentine's party!" If he were any more pleased with himself he'd do a dance.

Ramona puts the tray back down. "The alternative Valentine's party?"

"Yeah. No flowers. No chocolates. No sappy songs. And I know some great movies about relationships that don't have happy endings."

"Oh, I get it! The anti-Valentine's party!" She claps her hands together. "That is a fantastic idea! For all of us who aren't going to find our mailboxes stuffed with cards." Just the thing to cheer up someone whose heart is bruised if not actually broken. "No schmaltz. Or any of that lovey-dovey crap. Clear-sighted, cool-headed, and hard-hearted realism." She claps her hands again. "Oh, I know! I'll make heart cookies and break them all in half. And Josh can play some of his more depressing songs. God knows he has enough of them." She gives Sal a quick, excited hug. "Maybe I should make a banner that says 'Romance Sucks.'"

Sal's been carrying the torch for Ramona for so long it's a miracle it hasn't burned him. He wasn't going to say anything. Not today, not now. Ever since he found out Josh isn't interested in Ramona, he's thought about it. But, like Josh, he's never found the right moment; there's always been a good reason to wait for a better time. It's the hug that does it. The hug shoves him off his safe shelf of silence.

"Let's not get carried away," says Sal. "Romance can be cool. I think—" He suddenly looks around. "Where's your mother?"

"My mother?" Ramona looks around, too, as if Jade might swing down from the ceiling at any second. "She's in the back. Why? You want me to get her?"

Christ, no. That's the last thing he wants.

"No. No, I just—It's just that—" Sal takes a step toward her. "That—you know I like you, Ramona. . . ."

"Of course. I like you, too." And as soon as she says that she knows that isn't what he means. She needs to stop him from going any further. "We're friends."

Sal shakes his head. "No, I mean, really like you. I—"

"Sal." She puts a hand on his arm. "I really like you, too. But as a friend. I—" Ramona glances toward the door but of course no one's coming in to interrupt them. The world has pretty much stopped turning for a few seconds.

"It's okay." He moves away from her hand. "I get it. I didn't really think—I hoped, well, wished more. But I didn't really think . . . I—I guess I'd better go."

"Wait a minute. Don't get all funny on me." She grabs hold of him again. "It's just that I have kind of a crush on someone. So I'm kind of not open to anyone else. But I sure as hell know how it feels." She smiles, a sour, anti-Valentine's smile. "Really shitty."

Sal smiles back. "Yeah. You do know how it feels." He laughs. "But you know . . . If you ever change your mind . . ."

She gives him another quick hug. "You'll be the first to know."

He nods. "I'm not going to ask."

"You probably don't have to," says Ramona.

"You're going to do what?" It's possible that he misheard her; Mo can't have said what he thinks she said. "Did you say you're having a Valentine's Day party?"

St. Valentine's Day is a holiday beloved by the purveyors of greeting cards, chocolates, and roses—as well as by those who are either hopelessly romantic or lucky enough to know that they're going to receive cards, chocolates, and roses—but not everyone feels a thrill of excitement as February shuffles onto the calendar and hearts and cupids appear in shop windows.

Indeed, many people feel an overwhelming urge to go back to bed until it's all over. Josh has always been as indifferent to the day as a person who lives on a tropical island is indifferent to the difficulties of winter in Iceland — it has nothing to do with him. Until now, that is. Now, with the impending dumping of Simon Copeland — and against all odds — it did have something to do with him. It was going to be the day he sent his first-ever valentine to someone who isn't his mother or his cat. It was to be sent to Jena anonymously and with the printed message *From your Secret Admirer.* And when she told him about it and wondered who could have sent it, he was going to say, "Who do you think?" In a way that made sure she didn't think he meant the Un-incredible Hulk. And then, depending on how she reacted to that (a blush and knowing smile or the look of a girl who's just seen a zombie at the kitchen window) he would either blurt out the truth or make a joke. But Jena didn't break up with Simon (knock me over with a dust mote), and so instead of being the day Josh finally steps out of the closet of secret love, this year Valentine's will be the day Simon Copeland gives chocolates, a card and at least one red rose to Jenevieve Capistrano and takes her to the Parsons Falls High School St. Valentine's dance. Never mind going back to bed; a cave in the

Himalayas wouldn't be far enough away from Parsons Falls to allow Josh to forget what day it is.

"Not *me*, *we*," Ramona corrects him. "*We* are going to have the alternative Valentine's Day party."

"Alternative? Isn't the alternative to St. Valentine's April Fool's Day?"

She sighs. "Okay, not alternative, anti."

"What? We give each other thorns, empty candy wrappers, and poison-pen letters?"

"I was a little skeptical at first, too. But think about it. It's actually a pretty cool idea."

"I'm not being skeptical." He tries to be, but sometimes lately—the world being as it is—it's really hard to keep up. "I'm just trying to understand what it is."

If the Olympics had an event for sighing, Ramona Minamoto would be the favorite to win. "It's just a party for people who don't get all dewy-eyed every time they hear a song with 'I love you' in the lyrics, that's all." And for people who suspect that the phrase *lucky in love* will never apply to them—but she doesn't say that.

"You mean for the unlovable," says Josh.

She makes her camel-about-to-spit face. "We're not unlovable, it's just that no one's noticed how wonderful we are yet." Her smile makes up in teeth what it lacks in sweetness. "'None so blind as those who will not see . . .'" she adds in a mumble.

Josh doesn't really hear her. He's still coming to grips with the idea of a party. Apparently, it was Sal's idea, but Ramona thinks it's a great one. How is that possible? Didn't Sal say the only party he was interested in was the one to celebrate his first Oscar? And wasn't she the girl who locked herself in her room and refused to come out at the party to celebrate her twelfth birthday? Has he finally stepped through a wormhole and into a parallel world?

"And where are *we* going to have it?" Not at the Minamotos', which looks a lot like the gallery, only with more furniture. Carver has too many sisters. The Shines' place is too small unless Josh's mother goes out, when it's still too small, but at least they wouldn't have Hannah sitting in the middle of them trying to read.

"At Sal's." *Of course.* "He has the rec room."

"And who all's coming?" Together they don't have enough friends for a game of touch football.

She makes another of her Olympic-gold sighs. "For God's sake, Josh, who do you think's coming? This isn't the anti-prom. We're just talking about us. And maybe one or two other people. To balance the numbers."

She sounds so casual that he's immediately suspicious.

"Balance the numbers? What other people? Do you mean you're inviting some girls?"

"Do you have a problem with that, Joshua? I was under the impression that you like girls. At least some of them." Not only is Ramona a champion sigher, but she also has supercilious covered on a professional level. "It's not like dates or anything. No one's going to make you play spin the bottle. God forbid." She screws up her mouth, as if reluctant to let her next words out. "What I was thinking was I'd invite Zara." Zara makes sense. Lately she's been around a lot anyway. "And Murray Schneider."

"Murray Schneider? I didn't know you even talked to Murray Schneider."

"There's a lot about me you don't seem to know." Which, apparently, is his fault. "Anyway, I do talk to her. She's in the drama club."

"She is?" Murray Schneider is so shy that there are people who've gone to school with her since kindergarten who have never heard her voice. "In the drama club?" As what? A prop?

More sighing and rolling of eyes. "She's not the lead, Josh. She's a stagehand. You know, like your pal Jena? They also serve who only shove the sets around."

Whenever Ramona mentions Jena she sounds like she's criticizing.

"And you think Murray will come? Really? Does she know Carver'll be there? You do remember how mad she got when he told her Jonah didn't really live in a whale."

That was in middle school. Murray was so upset that she ran from the room in tears, opened the door too quickly, hit herself in the head with it, and passed out.

"I'm pretty sure she got over it," says Ramona. "Anyway, she won't be coming for Carver, she'll be coming for Sal. She'd probably apologize to Carver for what happened if Sal asked her to. She'd do anything for Sal."

"She would?" He has always thought of Sal as being as unlikely to incite passion as Josh; the Stay Puft Marshmallow Man to Josh's elf. At least Josh has a chin.

"Well, yeah. He's the reason she joined the drama club. She's a fool for love." Ramona's whole face shrugs. "Another one."

He doesn't ask her what she means; he thinks he knows.

"What about Carver?"

"What about him? He's okay hanging out with Zara. I'm not a dating service, you know. I just reckon it can't hurt to give Murray and Sal a chance to get to know each other better. They have a lot in common."

"They do?" Sal is Sal, large and loud, all waving arms and energy; Murray is small and quiet, a steady purr to the explosion that is Armando Salcedo.

"Yes, they do. Not obviously, maybe. But they're both clever and full of ideas. In a lot of ways they're really pretty similar."

Who'd have thought?

"It sounds like a dating service to me."

As so many before her have, she ignores him.

"So what do you think about the party? Sal says he knows some movies that would be perfect."

"Like what? *The St. Valentine's Day Massacre*?"

And it's another gold medal for Ramona Minamoto, who has beaten the previous world record by five thousand sighs!

"You know," says Ramona, "sarcasm isn't always the appropriate response. Not to everything. What Sal means are movies where the love story doesn't work out or ends really badly. You know. Like in life."

Josh nods. He can definitely identify with that.

"And I'm going to bake broken-heart cookies." Although he doesn't know it, Ramona can identify with that. "We think you should be in charge of the music because you know so many blues songs where love goes hideously wrong."

Does he ever. Though it should probably be called the blacks, not the blues. Dark as tar at the bottom of a two-hundred-foot well. The medley of songs Josh is beginning to think of as the soundtrack to his life starts running through his head. Ray Charles . . . Eric Von Schmidt . . . Roy Orbison . . . Linda Ronstadt . . . B. B. King . . . Leadbelly . . . Billie Holiday . . . Charley Patton . . . the Everly Brothers . . . Blind Willie McTell . . . Conway Twitty . . . Rolf Cahn . . . the Reverend Gary Davis . . . It's a list as long as the Mississippi. Longer.

"So you're up for it?"

As if he's had a better offer.

"It means I may have to break a few hearts myself to come, but sure, why not?"

"Great." This time her smile is small but happy. "And if you want, I'll bring my fiddle and we can play a couple of songs."

"I thought you play the violin."

"Not when I play with you," says Ramona.

Close Encounters of the Third Kind

Shopping bags hanging from them like ornaments on a Christmas tree, Jena and Tilda weave their way along the busy lower concourse of the mall to the west exit. Tilda, who has the enviable ability of being able to do two things at once, is checking her phone messages and talking about how high her father's blood pressure is going to go when he sees how much she's spent today. "He doesn't get how important this is," Tilda is saying. This is the first Valentine's Day that she and Jena have had steady boyfriends, which makes it a historic occasion. "I have to have the perfect dress to wear to the dance. And the purple dress is totally perfect. I mean, really, what if I hadn't found it?" Her bags swing with emotion. "I wouldn't be able to go, that's what. I'd rather stay home crying myself into a coma than wear second best." Because her eyes are on her phone, it isn't until she steps through the doors and into the cold that she realizes that she's alone. She turns around.

Jena is still inside, her face the human equivalent of a collapsed bridge. "We have to go back," says Jena. "You're right. It has to be perfect. And the blue dress isn't. I should never've bought it." The blue is second best. Possibly third best. "The green was way more flattering."

Always happy to be told she's right, Tilda comes back through the doors. "All I can say is, thank God you realized before we got all the way home." An event that has happened more than once, and not always because it was Jena who changed her mind.

Despite the fact that they haven't made it all the way home before Jena caught her mistake, there is still a problem.

Jena scans the directory near the door. "Can you remember which shop it was in?"

Tilda groans. They've been here so long and been in so many stores—often more than once and all of them selling very similar things—that by now they've melded into one giant, fluorescent-lighted emporium, identifiable only by the color of their bags. "Oh God, can't you?"

"I'm pretty sure it was upstairs," decides Jena.

They go upstairs. First they try the store Jena thinks is the right one, then they try the one Tilda is pretty sure is where they saw the green dress.

After four attempts, they decide they should be searching downstairs after all.

The green dress is in the last store they try. Jena grabs it from the rack with a cry of glee. "Oh, yes! This is so the right dress. Come on, I better try it on again."

Jena leads the way, going over all the reasons why the green dress is so much better than the blue, and Tilda follows, busy with her phone again as her finger flies over the screen. As the changing room comes into view, Jena comes to another sudden stop. She blinks, unable to believe her eyes. "Oh my God," she says. "There's Josh."

It is Josh, standing a few feet from the entrance and surrounded by Ladies' Leisurewear, staring into the distance as if he's waiting for a bus. Except for a small boy scuffing after his mother, tears in his eyes, Josh is the only male in sight.

"Jesus Christ," says Tilda. "What the hell is he doing here?" And then, in case Jena still needs some convincing, adds, "Didn't I tell you he's weird?"

Josh hates clothes shopping; he'd rather play hockey, and he'd rather break his hands and never be able to pick up a guitar again than play hockey. Not only is shopping boring and stressful, but because of his height (or lack of it) hassled shoppers often think he is a clear path and walk right into him. One Christmas he was actually knocked to the ground in the mall; he was lucky the only thing that was broken were his glasses. Online shopping may literally have saved his life.

The reason Josh is loitering outside the women's changing room of this particular store at this particular time on this particular day is a long story, but the short version is that Carver's youngest sister, Talita, was promised a shopping trip today, and Carver was the only family member who could take her. Carver was desperate. "You have to come, man," insisted Carver. "I'd rather work for one of the big oil companies than go by myself. You're like my brother. We have to share the pain." But, in the end, it was Talita's pain Josh chose to share. She didn't want to go by herself either. "You know what Carver's like," said Talita. "Anything you look at, he has to tell you how bad the company that made it is. It takes all the fun out. If you come, too, he'll talk to you and leave me alone."

That there is no sign of either Carver or Talita at the moment is because Carver has gone to the men's room (possibly the one at the end of the universe) and Talita is in the changing room, trying things on very slowly. Josh wishes one or both of them would hurry up. This isn't somewhere you would think to look for a teenage boy. He feels like the only duck on the lake on the first day of hunting season. Shoppers and saleswomen keep glancing at him. Suspiciously. Giving him odd looks, wondering what he's up to, guessing it's nothing good. His only consolation is that there's no chance of running into anyone he knows.

And then, of course, he does. Or they run into him.

He hears someone laugh nearby. It's a familiar laugh, one he's been hearing since grade school, often aimed at him or his friends—and one that makes his heart drop down to the soles of his shoes. Maybe Tilda doesn't see him. Maybe she isn't with Jena. Maybe she'll walk right by. He doesn't want to look over; he wants the floor to open like a giant jaw and swallow him whole. But the floor doesn't, and he does.

Tilda does see him, she is with Jena and they are moving toward him like a tank—a tank bedecked with balloons.

"Josh!" cries Jena. "What are you doing here?"

This may be the first time that Tilda Kopel has ever made actual eye contact with him, as if she's making eye contact with a tree. And she doesn't speak to him, of course. "He can't be waiting for his girlfriend," she says to Jena.

Jena doesn't exactly laugh, but she doesn't exactly not laugh, either. She does blush.

To her, Josh says, "I'm here with Carver and his little sister. She has birthday money to spend."

"Oh, that's nice," says Jena.

"Are they invisible?" mutters Tilda.

"Only Carver's invisible," Josh tells Jena. "Talita's inside trying stuff on."

"That's where we're going." Jena holds up the green dress, and the two bags she's holding in the same hand. "What do you think? It's for the dance."

Tilda mumbles something else, but this time too softly for him to catch what it is.

He's tempted to ask *What dance?*—but since he really wants them to go away, or at least for Tilda to go away—what he says is, "It's nice."

"I hope so." She sways slightly. "I mean, it is for Valentine's. I know you think I'm a big sap, but I think romance rules—and this is going to be the most romantic night I've ever had." Tilda shuffles beside her, and Jena says, "Hey, do you think you could do me a favor? Could you look after my bags while I try the dress on?" All of her smiles are good, but this one's very good. "I'll only be, like, five minutes. Promise. And since you're standing here anyway . . ."

When he returns to find Josh surrounded by Jena and Tilda's shopping bags, Carver looks from the bags to Josh. "Do I take it Jena Capistrano's in the building?"

Josh jerks his head toward the changing room. "She's in there."

Carver sighs. "Dude," he says, "you never learn."

The Resurrection of Hope

"This time I really mean it." This time Jena really looks as if she really means it. No tears. No sparks. No drama. No woman of passion throwing emotions around like confetti. Today her voice has all the feeling of a block of ice. "No way am I ever going to have anything to do with Simon Copeland again — so long as I live. It is done. Over. If I never see him again it'll be way too soon."

Josh shakes his head as though trying to clear it. "It's the damndest thing, Jen, but I'm having this déjà vu moment. It's like I feel as if you've said this before."

Jena, however, is not in a laughing mood right now. She is really serious. "You have heard it before. I know that, Josh. But you have my word as the daughter of a general in the United States Army that you will never hear it again." She makes an *X* in the air over her chest. "Cross my heart and hope to grow a beard. I don't care if

Simon crawls over broken glass to apologize, we are once and forever through. Dead as the dinosaurs. Deader."

"You're upset," says Josh, even as, vampire-like, Hope climbs out of its coffin and snuggles up beside him. Tapping its toes. Waiting. "When you calm down—"

"I am calm." She is; she could only be calmer if she'd been turned to stone. "I know I can be a little superficial sometimes . . ." Something Simon has pointed out to her, and he should know. "But Simon's not so awesomely good-looking or popular that he can get away with being such a jerk forever. Everything comes to an end sooner or later." This party-size bottle of soda is empty. "Tilda's not going to like it. You know, 'cause she wanted us to double for the prom in the spring. But that's the way it goes. Cookies crumble."

Josh would like to ignore Hope and its tapping toes—it's screwed him over before—but nonetheless hears himself say, "Is this for real? You're not going to change your mind five minutes from now? You really mean it this time?"

"Totally. The only word I want to hear from Simon Copeland is good-bye. When you hear what he did you'll get it."

This last fight introduced a new and deeper dimension to their disagreements. Simon went into nuclear meltdown because Jena was talking to another boy.

"Talking?" Maybe Simon got a head injury in one of his games that's gone undiagnosed. "You talk to me all the time."

But Simon isn't jealous of Josh. Josh threatens him about as much as a cotton ball. Simon is, however, jealous of Lucas Adamani. Lucas Adamani is of the same species as Simon. He's good-looking, is part of Tilda's crowd, and is captain of the Parsons Falls varsity football team.

A bunch of them were hanging out at Starbucks, and Jena wound up sitting next to Lucas. Simon said that she ignored him completely and gave all her attention to Lucas. Simon said that she and Lucas were flirting. He'd never been so embarrassed in his life.

"Flirting! Can you believe it? That's what Simon thinks of me! That right in front of him I'd flirt with someone else? Have we met? We were talking. That's all we were doing." Which is what she said to Simon. Talking. T-a-l-k-i-n-g. "Which, in case he hadn't noticed, is what people do. It's what separates them from other animals." That and shopping and weapons of mass destruction. "Simon said that talking isn't the only thing people do." He said it in a sneering, leering way. "For God's sake, I've known Lucas longer than I've known Simon Copeland. He's been friends with Tilda since before she had her nose job. So, you know, I have talked to him before."

Though not, perhaps, when Simon was around.

"And then he said that if I like talking to Lucas so much I can go to the freakin' Valentine's dance with him." Jena reminded him that Lucas has a girlfriend. And Simon said that was a real coincidence, since Jena used to have a boyfriend. "I couldn't believe what I was hearing. I swear, if we'd been standing on a bridge I would've pushed him off."

Josh has always been careful not to say anything even vaguely negative about Simon, but now—with Simon finally about to have the door slammed behind him—he breaks his own rule. "He has always been kind of controlling."

And immediately remembers why he had the rule in the first place.

"Controlling?" She shakes her head. "Simon's not controlling, Josh. He's behaving like a pig-headed, jealous idiot, but that's because he cares about me so much. Not because he always has to run the show."

You could've fooled me.

"I just meant—" He breaks off. He meant that Simon always has to have things his way. Fortunately, she's not really in conversational mode.

"Not that I'm going to be swayed by that," Jena steams on. "I've had all I'm going to take of his moodiness and his temper and him putting me last."

Josh believes her. The blindfold of love has been torn from her eyes, and at last she sees Simon for what he is: a handsome, athletic, and charming waste of time. A demanding bully in the clothing of a prince.

"So?" says Josh. The dance is two days away. "What happens now?" He laughs so she'll know he's joking. "Assuming you're not going to the Valentine's hoedown with Lucas and his girlfriend."

This time she manages a small but bitter smile. "It would serve Simon right if I did. But I'm not doing that, am I?" She shrugs. *What can you do?* "Cinderella, there's no way you're going to the ball." She sighs. "Why couldn't I fall for someone reliable and considerate?"

"Don't ask me," says Josh.

"Some romantic evening," says Jena. "Sitting at home watching *The Great Escape* with my dad for the nine hundredth time."

"There's no need for anything that drastic," says Josh. "You still have me."

To Do or Not to Do

"Enough is enough," Josh tells himself. He's flip-flopped, vacillated, and waffled for longer than it takes to hand-build a guitar. He has to be the greatest procrastinator since Hamlet. No, yes, maybe. Should I? Shouldn't I? What if? If only . . . But no more. Jena is through with Simon, and Josh is through with indecision and fear. His self stares back at him from the mirror, looking not nearly as confident as Josh would like, and behind his self he can see Charley Patton stretched out on the bed like a draft stopper, watching him with his inscrutable gold eyes. "I mean it," says Josh. "This time I'm going to tell her." Saying the words out loud makes them true. He really does mean it; he really is going to do it. Charley Patton yawns.

To strengthen his commitment, Josh tells Carver.

Carver looks as if he's been listening to an oil

executive explaining the win-win benefits of Arctic drilling. "Seriously? You're really going to do it? No more shilly-shallying?"

Josh nods. "I shilly-shally no more. It's risky. But I've given it a lot of thought, and, logically, there's not a better time than Valentine's Day. Love is in the air and everything. The mood of the moment will be in my favor."

"Valentine's being the best window for this doesn't sound like logic to me," says Carver. "It sounds like a superstition. Lucky number. Lucky shirt." He points a tortilla chip at Josh. "Remember when Talita was really little and she carried that toy rabbit with her everywhere because she thought it was good luck? And then she got it caught in the spokes of my mom's bike and nearly killed them both. That's what comes of relying on luck."

"So you think I shouldn't go for it?"

"I didn't say that." Carver is feeling some compassion fatigue; if he'd been Horatio he would have been tempted to kill Hamlet himself. "You know I don't think she's going to take the chance of being dropped by Tilda to date you. But I still think you should do it. You have to get some closure on this or you'll drive yourself crazy." And everybody else. "Only, if you ask me, what you need are My Little Pony girl and God in your favor, not the mood of the moment."

"I'm kind of surprised you're not being even more negative," says Josh. "I thought you frown on things like girlfriends and relationships for anyone who doesn't have an advanced degree."

"Not for everyone. Mainly for me. And it's not like I don't have feelings. But you know . . ." He smiles. Ruefully. "Girls think I'm odd—"

"Don't be modest," says Josh. "Everybody thinks you're odd."

"You didn't let me finish my sentence. They think I'm odd. I figure I'll need at least two sets of letters after my name to attract anyone. But girls like you."

They do? How come Josh never noticed that?

"Not all girls," says Carver. "Just the ones who are into funky musicians."

Two opinions are better than one, especially when the one is not as enthusiastic as you might have wanted.

The next person Josh tells is Sal.

"You're going to tell her how you feel?" Sal sounds as if a better idea might be to tell her how someone else feels. Preferably someone she doesn't know and will never meet.

"I thought you were all for love and taking a chance."

"Yeah." Sal shrugs. "I was. But now I'm not so sure. . . ."

"I'm not going straight in the deep end," says Josh.

"I thought I'd ask her out first and if she doesn't drop dead on the spot I'll take it from there."

Sal shakes his head. "I don't want to be discouraging, but . . . you know . . . I have to say that, if I'm really honest, I don't think you should do it." He sighs. "Not unless you're prepared to get hit by the juggernaut of rejection and end up as roadkill on the highway of love."

"How come? What happened to boldly going? Having an adventure?"

"Yeah, well, that was before I went boldly myself," says Sal. If he were a porcupine he'd have rolled himself into a ball by now. "I'm speaking from experience here. Unhappy experience. Been there. Done that. And I think if she hasn't given you some really clear message—you know, like asking you out or tattooing your name on her arm—then I think you should keep your mouth shut. Once you say it, you can't take it back."

Josh stopped absorbing anything Sal was saying after "speaking from experience." "You? You asked somebody out?" He couldn't mean Murray Schneider, because Murray Schneider would have said yes. "Who?"

Sal looks at him as if he's forgotten his lines. "Well, who do you think? Marilyn Monroe?"

"I don't have a clue. I didn't know you were interested in anybody."

Apparently Josh makes everybody sigh like that.

"You know, you're becoming the walking definition of self-absorbed. Wake up, man, and smell the hormones," says Sal. "It's pretty obvious. You can't be that oblivious."

Oh, but he can.

"So who is it?"

"It's not exactly a big mystery." Or only to Josh. "It's Ramona." The "of course" is unspoken but understood. "She's . . . You know. She's awesome."

"You asked out Ramona?" The "Minamoto?" is also unspoken but understood. "But—you're just friends." She said they were just friends.

"Yeah, well, that's the thing, isn't it? We are just friends. But that's not my choice."

For some reason he feels almost betrayed. Why doesn't anybody ever tell him anything? "I knew you were seeing more of each other. Because of the play . . ." And for some other reason he feels irrationally (and uncharitably) glad that she turned Sal down.

"Are you so surprised because it's Ramona, or are you so surprised because it's me?" asks Sal.

"Well, I . . ." He has no idea.

"It can't be because it's Ramona," says Sal. "She's unquestionably attractive." He gives Josh another why-can't-you-learn-your-lines? look. "Except to you, I guess."

"Hang on," says Josh. "Is that why you joined the drama club? Because of Mo?"

"Shit, man, you really do live in a parallel world, don't you? Why did you think I joined?"

"To broaden your directorial experience?"

"That's not really the experience I wanted to broaden. I wanted to be around Ramona."

"You're always around her."

"Yeah, but you know . . ." Can Sal possibly be blushing? Is that something future award-winning directors do? Would Orson Welles blush? Would Alexander Payne? Surely not Wes Anderson. "Without you being there, too. And I wanted to have something to talk about that was just between her and me."

Sometimes Josh watches *Antiques Roadshow* with his mother. He is having an *Antiques Roadshow* moment, feeling like someone who brought in an old vase that's been in the attic filled with paper clips for the last ninety years because nobody liked it — only to discover that it's a work of art and worth a small fortune.

"So you actually asked her out?"

"I didn't get that far. I started out by telling her I liked her." Sal makes a face. *Stupid or what?* "And I've never been so scared shitless in my life. I thought I was going to faint."

"And?"

"What do you mean 'and'? And we're going to elope to Las Vegas as soon as we finish high school." Sal sighs. "She was as nice as you can be when you're stabbing some poor jerk in the heart. She said she really likes me a lot, but just as friends." He fiddles with the cuff of his shirt. "Actually, she was very sympathetic. Said she knows what it feels like. She's been there, too. She said she gave me points for saying something because she's never had the nerve."

"Really? Mo? Mo *likes* likes somebody?" This is a lot to take in. Some girls are desperate to have a boyfriend, but Ramona's never been like that. She's never declared any feelings for anyone who isn't a dead composer, a character in a book, or a domestic pet. "She told me she's never been into anyone."

"She did?" Sal considers this for a few seconds. Or possibly it's Josh he's considering. It's hard to tell. "So you think she just said that so I didn't cry in front of her?"

"No." Josh shrugs. He shakes his head. He doesn't seem to know what to do with his hands. "I don't know. I'm only repeating what she said." What did she say? She said no. She'd never been interested in anyone. *Not really.* He didn't know what she meant and she said it meant *not really.* When she was little. Only now does he wonder if she was telling the truth. Why wouldn't Mo tell him the truth? "It must be one of the post-postmodernists . . . maybe that tall guy with the black hair. I know they go to exhibitions together. What's his name? Dara or Darius. Something like that. Artsy-fartsy and full of himself." He looks at Sal, as if he'd forgotten he was there. "I don't suppose she said who it is."

Sal shakes his head. "Not really."

He has no intention of telling Ramona about his plans, but he does have to tell her not to bring her fiddle to the Valentine's party. Fair's fair.

"You have got to be joking." Her voice is like a punch. "What do you mean, you're not coming Saturday?"

He should have texted. There's a lot to be said for the impersonal electronic message. For one thing, you can't tell how mad the recipient is.

"I'm really sorry, Mo. I just can't."

"But I've been practicing 'Some of These Days.' I know it's one of your favorites." No eye contact being another advantage of the e-mail or text. "Why can't you come?"

He could tell her Charley Patton's sick. Or that he doesn't want his mom to be alone, missing his dad. Or even that the band got a last-minute gig. But he doesn't. He's pretty sure she'd know he was lying.

"It's Jena. She and Simon had a big fight—"

"Excuse me!" Ramona pulls out her phone. "Just give me a minute while I make the announcement on Twitter. This is, like, earth-shattering news. Nobody's going to believe it! We have to alert the President! They'll probably call a special session of the UN!"

He should have lied.

Josh holds up a hand. "Okay, okay. You're very funny. I know they're always breaking up, but this time it's the real deal. This time she's not going to change her mind. They're officially over."

"And what exactly does that have to do with you?" If scorn were water, he'd be drowning.

"I said I'd hang out with her. She doesn't want to be alone." Ramona's expression doesn't change. "You can understand that. It's Valentine's. Being alone would make her feel like the last teddy bear left on the toy store shelf on Christmas Eve."

"And what about *your* friends? Your other friends, I mean. What about how we feel?"

"Yeah, but you have each other."

She leans back in her chair. Regrouping. "I still don't see why you can't come," she says. "Bring Jena with you. More the merrier. She and Murray can talk about scene changes."

He did think of that. Not Jena swapping stagehand

stories with Murray, but her going to Sal's with him. But when he told Jena about the alternative Valentine's Day party she said, "That would really show Simon, wouldn't it?" He could tell she was being sarcastic. She didn't say it in so many words, but he got the impression that she'd rather hang out with her dad and his poker buddies than with Josh's friends. What she did say, with so much sweetness and sincerity that you had to wonder why she thought she can't act, was that she's sure they're really interesting and terrific people and everything but she'd feel uncomfortable. She couldn't even imagine what they'll do at this party. Josh said they'll play pin the tail on the donkey and then shoot cans off the fence in the backyard with BB guns. It was a few seconds before Jena said, "Oh, that's funny. No, really, what'll they do?" Josh said hang out. Maybe watch a movie. Ramona and he might play a little music. He could tell from the way she smiled that she thought that was kind of weird. "See what I mean?" said Jena. "We don't do that kind of thing at the parties I go to." She wasn't being mean, she said, but his friends aren't really her crowd. "I mean, you don't hang out with my crew, do you?" Not that he's ever been invited. "Because, you know, you wouldn't fit. And I wouldn't fit with yours." She laughed. "Can you imagine me trying to have a conversation with them? With

Carver? *How's global warming coming along?* And I hear Sal and Ramona blah-blahing away in drama meetings and half the time I don't have a clue what they're talking about."

"I don't think she's really up for a lot of people," he says to Ramona now. "You know, dented heart and everything."

Ramona tilts her head to one side. Considering—though he isn't certain what. "So you think this time she and the football hero are really quits? That's what you think?"

"Looks like it." And then, because she is still watching him consideringly, answers the question she doesn't ask—the one he wasn't going to answer. "I figure maybe I'll say something."

"You mean, before she gets another boyfriend," says Ramona.

The Trouble with Hope

Though this is something else she hasn't said in so many words, Josh can tell that Jena thinks he's all head and no heart: emotionally contained and as romantic as cold mashed potatoes. Well, she's going to have to think again. If she wants romance she's going to get romance. Josh's mother is out for the evening, so he has the house to himself and doesn't have to explain what he's doing or beg her to stay in her room — no matter what. He went online and looked up romantic movies, and downloaded three of them. He bought enough candles to torch Rome and burned himself several times lighting them. Instead of boring old pretzels and chips, he got olives and those corn nut things Jena likes. He's not sure why, but olives seem very sexy to him, even though he doesn't particularly like to eat them. He bought a single red rose. He's rehearsed what he's going to say so many times you'd think he was addressing Congress. He cut himself shaving, changed his shirt three times, and has a record ready to play that will tell her everything she needs to know even before he opens his mouth. Ray Charles singing that classic of unrequited love "You Don't Know Me," about someone who's always been just a friend to the woman he loves.

By six thirty, when Jena should be nearing his street, Josh is so nervous he thinks he may be having a stroke. It could happen. Youth protects you from nothing, except maybe taxes. *Be calm . . . be calm . . .* he tells himself. He doesn't want her to arrive only to find his lifeless body on the living room floor. Not now, for God's sake. How ironic would that be? He turns on the music when he hears the bell, picks up the rose, and takes several deep breaths. He wipes his hands on his jeans and breathes some more. The bell rings again. Damn, there aren't any lights on in the living room. What if she doesn't notice the flickering candlelight and thinks he forgot she's coming over? Josh dashes into the hall and trips over Charley Patton, who howls indignantly. He'll be lucky not to kill himself before he gets to the door.

As soon as he opens it, he wishes he hadn't.

Jena looks like she's stepped out of a dream. She's all dressed up: new dress, new shoes, and her good coat.

The dream she's stepped out of is not his, of course. Without even looking he can see Copeland's car at the curb. Jena's going to the dance.

Josh hides the rose behind his back and steps forward, blocking her view into the house.

"You didn't have to dress up for me," Josh jokes. He hopes she doesn't realize he's wearing his best shirt, the one he only wears for gigs, and his lucky red suspenders that belonged to his dad.

"Oh, Josh . . ." Jena makes a sad, apologetic face. "I'm really sorry. I tried to call you but it went straight to voice mail."

He turned off his phone so he wouldn't forget to turn it off; he didn't want them to be disturbed.

"I'm guessing you and Simon made up." If he holds the doorframe any more tightly he'll break it.

"Yeah. You know . . ." Her shrug is helpless. As if it's something that happened to her, like getting a cold. "I just can't seem to stay mad at him for long."

"Fool for love," says Josh, trying to remember where he heard that.

Jena laughs. "I guess that's me. But there are worse things, right?"

There definitely are worse things, even if he can't think of any of them at the moment.

He doesn't feel angry or particularly surprised. More like he's been standing in the cold for several hours, waiting for a train that isn't going to come. *None so blind as those who will not see*, he thinks—but can't remember where he heard that either.

"Well, have a great time." Josh nods toward the road. "You better go. You don't want to keep Simon waiting. Not tonight."

She's peering under his arm. "Why is it so dark?" She sniffs. "What's that smell?"

"Nothing." Lilac. Lavender. Jasmine. Rose. Sandalwood. "Some candles my mom had."

"It looks like Christmas or something in there."

Could be. It definitely seems to be snowing in his heart.

"It's just some candles my—"

Jena pushes past him and into the hall, her eyes following the shimmering flames, a string of light weaving its way through the room. She turns back to him. "What's going on?"

"Nothing," says Josh. "I just wanted it to look Valentiney, that's all. I thought it would cheer you up."

But she isn't listening to Josh. "Who's that singing? What's that song?"

"No one." Thank God she doesn't know much music

that wasn't made in the last five years. "Just one of my old records."

Her smile isn't sure of itself. "You did all this for *me*?"

Who else? The dozen other people he's expecting?

"Yeah. Like I said, I thought it would cheer you up."

Outside, Simon leans out the car window and calls, "Hey, Jen! We have to get going!"

For once, Josh wishes she would do what Simon says. Go. Quickly.

"You really should go." He tries to edge her back to the door. "Simon's waiting."

"Josh, I—I'm really sorry. I didn't think—"

"It's okay." If he wasn't holding the rose behind his back and had two hands free he'd be tempted to just grab hold of her and throw her out of the house. "I figured you'd probably change your mind. I just did the candles in case."

"I really am sorry. I didn't know you'd go to all this trouble."

He doesn't want her to be sorry; he wants her to leave. "It's fine. I told you." He gives her a tug, but she seems to have grown roots.

"You're such a good friend," says Jena. "Next to Tilda, you're the best friend I've ever had. You know that, don't you?"

Of course he does. He's always known it; she made it

clear that she would never be interested in him as a boyfriend; made it clear they'd always only be friends. But he wouldn't listen. Not to her, not to himself, and not to anyone. That's the problem with Hope; it blinds you even more than love.

She gestures to the room. "I just feel so bad—"

She's not the only one.

"It's okay, Jen. Really." It is. It has to be. She never meant to hurt him or lead him on. He's brought this on himself. She always said she was nothing like him; he always knew what kind of boyfriend she wanted, and the boyfriend she wanted was never Josh. Jena doesn't want to be on the sidelines; she wants to be smack-dab in the middle with Simon Copeland or someone like him. Someone good-looking and popular and envied. Prom queen to his king. At the center of the high school universe with Tilda Kopel. And he remembers her once saying, *Sometimes the people you like the best aren't the ones you're attracted to.* "I swear."

"I really am sorry. . . ." She bites her bottom lip.

"For God's sake, Jena, it's okay. You have nothing to be sorry for." Unlike Josh.

Simon calls her name again. "I guess I better go." She gives him a hug. "Try not to burn the house down. I'll talk to you tomorrow."

Josh stands in the doorway, watching her run down the front path and get in the car. He waves as they pull away and even Simon waves back. The rose falls to the floor.

Back inside, he turns off the player and puts out the candles. He doesn't bother turning on the lights but throws himself on the sofa. Charley Patton jumps up beside him. Josh strokes his head. "Looks like it's you and me, boy." Charley nuzzles against him. Your friends are there when you need them most. Even if all they can do is purr. He and Charley sit in the dark, each lost in his own thoughts. Something Ramona said way long ago last year comes back to him: *Tilda Kopel would never allow it.* He paid no attention then, of course, but now he realizes how right Ramona was. Tilda Kopel never would allow it. If Jena had chosen to date Josh she would have lost everything else—Tilda and all her other new friends, feeling like she fit, finally belonging. Somehow, this makes him feel slightly less bad. The sudden ringing of the doorbell makes both him and Charley jump.

For only as long as it takes him to get to the door, Josh thinks it might be Jena. She dropped something. She forgot something. She changed her heart. But even as he puts his hand on the knob he knows it isn't her. He opens the door.

It's Ramona. She's all in black—black coat, black lace skirt, black boots, black hearts hanging from her ears—looming in front of him like the ghost of Valentine's to come. She doesn't wait for him to ask her in. She strides past him, stepping on the fallen flower. She has her violin strapped across her back.

"Christ," she says, "turn on a light before I trip over something."

He has no choice but to follow her in, kicking the rose into a corner and turning on a light. "What are you doing here?"

At the moment she's looking around the room. She squinches up her nose. "It smells like a florist. Or one of those New Age shops with all the crystals in the window."

"So what are you doing here?"

She turns to face him. "I saw Jena leave with Simon." Even her earrings seem to shrug. "So I figured they made up."

This is all he needs. A lecture from Ramona. "Look, I know what you're going to say. You told me so. You—"

"That's not what I'm going to say. I didn't come to make you feel worse. I came to get you. You know, for the party."

"The party?" He needs a party about as much as Charley Patton needs a skateboard. "But I—"

"No buts," says Ramona. "You're coming with me."

"I don't really feel—"

Ramona doesn't care. She's a lot more like her mother than he thought. "You're not sitting here by yourself in the dark all night. You're going to come and hang out with the rest of us. We're all in the same boat, Josh. You, me, Sal, Carver, Murray, and Zara. And it's not the love boat. So you're going to get your guitar and we're going to play some cool music and by the end of the night everybody's going to feel a lot better. You know, 'cause at least we have great songs and friends."

"I appreciate what you're trying to do, Mo—"

"I'm not trying. I'm doing it." She grabs him by the shoulders. Her eyes are darker than he thought, too. "You listen to me, Joshua Shine. I know you talked to Sal, so I know you know how great he's feeling. And how great I'm feeling. Really, if you want the truth, we all feel shitty. Maybe not as shitty as you're feeling right now, but bad enough. So get over yourself." She looks at the couch. "Back me up here, Charley. Don't you think I'm right?"

Charley Patton opens his eyes, stares at them both for a second, then closes his eyes again.

"That's a yes," says Ramona. "He doesn't want you hanging around here making him depressed." As she takes her hands from his shoulders, she gives him a shove. "Go get your guitar."

Some of These Days

After the days of dark and cold, finally spring has arrived. The sun is shining, the trees are budding, his mother's hyacinths are blooming, and Josh's world has gone back to how it was before last September. More or less.

The bleak midwinter is a good time to think. Sitting inside with your cat and your records and your guitar, while outside the freezing winds blow and the snow falls and the part of the world that doesn't depend on electricity lies low. Josh has done a lot of thinking, and a great deal of it has been about Ramona. How she's always been there for him. How many times they've laughed so much over something that he nearly stopped breathing. How she reacted when he asked her if she'd ever been interested in anyone. He got over Jena. He sees her in school and they're friendly, but he doesn't hang out with her anymore. Doesn't want to. She called him a couple of times—when Simon was away for the weekend, when Tilda was visiting her aunt—but he said he was busy. He doesn't miss her. But he'd miss Mo if she suddenly disappeared from his life. He'd miss her a lot. Sometimes you don't see what's right in front of you because you're looking at something else. That's when he finally started thinking about Ramona not as a sister but as a girl; when he understood the reason why it annoyed him that she was seeing so much of Sal was because he was jealous. Oblivious *and* jealous. What a combination.

Josh woke up on this Sunday morning to sunshine and Ramona on his mind. And here she is, sitting across from him with her after-yoga tea, talking about the play.

"So it was totally awesome. You should have heard the applause." *Bye Bye Birdie* had its out-of-town preview at the local nursing home, and was an unqualified success. "Everybody was great, and lots of people commented on the costumes, and Mr. Boxhill said he couldn't've done it without Sal, but, of course, Tilda thinks that most of the credit should go to her." She picks up her cup. "If it goes that well on the night of the actual performance, there'll be no living with her."

Josh carefully lifts the bag from his tea. "There's no living with her now."

"And can you imagine what she's going to be like at the cast party?" laughs Ramona. "She's going to think it's for her!"

"I forgot about the party," lies Josh. "So, who are you going with?" Every member of the drama club is allowed one guest. Sal's invited Carver. Murray's invited Zara. But Mo has yet to invite him. "Dara?"

She stares at him over her cup. Blankly. "Who?"

"Maybe it's not Dara. Maybe it's Darius." She continues to look like a new sheet of paper. "You know. Your friend with the black hair and the earring."

"You mean Dillon Sanduski?"

"Is that his name?"

She does the sigh, accompanied by the rolling eyes. "Yes, that's his name. For God's sake, Josh, you've met him, like, a hundred times."

"I think it was only ninety-nine."

She sets her cup very gently in its saucer. "I hadn't thought about it." Which is both true and not true. It's true that it never occurred to her to ask Dillon. But that's not because she hasn't thought about the party, it's because she thought it was obvious she'd go with Josh. She's noticed a change in him over the last month or so. Now he looks at her as though he really sees her. She was hoping he'd say something first. Give her a sign, make a move. "Maybe I will ask him." Or grow old waiting.

"Thing is," says Josh. "I mean, why I asked." He seems to be studying his spoon for signs of life. "I don't really think that would be a great idea."

"You don't?" She sweeps a few grains of sugar to the floor. "Why not?"

"Well . . ." Maybe he's thinking of writing a song about the endless fascination of a teaspoon. "I don't think he'd enjoy a party like that. He's such an art-school type."

Maybe she won't have to grow old waiting. "Do you have someone else in mind? Someone who would enjoy a party like that?"

"Well . . ."

She leans forward so she's almost half across the table. "Josh? Do you have someone else in mind?"

He puts down the spoon. "There's always me."

"You?" As if he's the last person she would consider.

"Yeah." And, with all the courage he never found before, he says, "You know. It could be our first real date."

"What makes you think I'd want to go out with you?" asks Ramona.

"I don't." Josh smiles. "I just hope you will."

She smiles back.